Comanche Rattle

ELIJAH BRUNSON

PAGE PUBLISHING, INC.
New York, NY

First originally published by Page Publishing, Inc. 2019

ISBN 978-1-64424-580-4 (Paperback)
ISBN 978-1-64424-581-1 (Digital)

Printed in the United States of America

Chapter 1

It was a warm spring evening at the cabin in the backwoods of Tennessee. There were always things that needed to be done around the farm, and each had jobs that needed to be done. The older girls had their chores, as did we, the two boys, while the baby played on the floor. Our mother sat at the table preparing things for the evening meal. Me and my younger brother, Jamie, enjoyed causing the girls all the trouble they could before heading out to do their evening chores.

I knew it was time to get my chores done; no time for playing around. I crossed the room and headed out the door. I could still hear Ma's voice as she followed me to the door.

"Jamie, stop pestering your sisters and tend to your chores. Matthew, it is your job to bring in the stock and close that gate tight. You leave it open again and you'll be the one rounding them up iffen they get loose again!"

"Yes, Ma! I'm going," I yelled back as I could hear her talking to the rest of the family.

"The rest of you listen to me, and I mean right now! Jamie, you and the baby need to get this mess cleaned up right now! You girls get busy with cooking supper!"

I could hear all these pleasant sounds as I marched down the hill and headed toward the creek in search of our little herd of cows. I was only thinking about getting my chores done, not death and destruction that was going to occur in the cabin. Those things were the furthest thing from my mind. I just had to get my job done.

I found myself thinking about Ma. She was a stickler for cleanliness and education with all of us. She even went so far as to go checking behind our ears at bedtime. I guessed that was why I think of Ma as a real lady. Yes, neatness always counted with her along with manners and being polite. One thing she never allowed was any cursing. Not a word of that kind. She said that she educated us so that we could converse with anyone without resorting to that type of language. It made me smile just thinking about Momma. She was a lady but one without all those frills about her. I loved her more than words could ever say.

I was just dragging my bare feet in the dirt of the lane as I got to the bottom of the hill. I had been taking my time when I could barely hear the beat of horse hooves rolling in front of the cabin. The problem was that I was too far away to see who it might be or what they were up to. Whoever they were, they didn't know I existed. The farther down the hollow I went, the harder it was to hear any sounds from the cabin.

Where we lived put town at least five miles away. There was some traffic usually in the morning and rarely in the evening, particularly at suppertime. Very rarely did anyone come down our lane from the main road. So it was without a thought that I plunged on down the hill to the last place that I had remembered seeing the cows.

Those cranky cows went as far as they could go before the timber fence stopped them. It took several minutes to gather them up and started heading them back toward the house. It was just as I bent to pick up a branch to shoo them when I was jerked from my daydreaming. What drilled into my ears were the sounds of guns being fired. Not only was it the sound of guns being fired but by the screams and yells of Mom and the girls.

I could hear the voices of the raiders as they were carried on the wind to me.

"Yi hi! Yi hi! Ain't this here fun, boys?"

Each yell was punctuated by another gunshot. Even the squealing pigs were silenced with the last of the gunshots.

"Hey, boss, you and Lane, hurry it up! Someone's liable to stop by after hearing all these gunshots. I told you two to get those two girls hog-tied and on those horses pronto. Let's get shut of this place! Boss, we got to go now, not tomorrow!"

All I could hear were the gunshots that cut through the evening air like thunderclaps to my ears. There was a final scream which ended as abruptly as if it had been cut off in midair by a knife.

Hearing all this, I began to run as fast as I could, knowing that I would be way too late to stop whatever had happened. Trying to scramble up the hill left me with fear and dread. The cows were forgotten as he ran stumbling with bursting lungs to the top of the hill. The rocks and stones meant nothing to bare feet as I rushed to the cabin. Rushing around the corner of the cabin, the distant rumbling and clatter of retreating hoofbeats could be heard going down the road.

Totally out of air, I bent over with my head down between my knees and my hands on my legs trying to get any breath back. Everything I saw was destroyed.

I began to search all the destruction that lay before me for any sign of life. The only things that I could see were dead animals everywhere. Chicken, pigs, sheep, and the old dog. Nothing was left alive. Everything we had was senselessly slaughtered. *Who would do such a thing?* It was a sight that I knew I would never be able to remove from my brain. Little did I realize the enormity of the destruction that had been committed on my family until I headed for the cabin.

Even as these thoughts raced through my mind, I took notice that a fire was licking away at the door to the cabin. It took only a moment for me to grab a bucket of water and doused the fire.

In a flash, I was terrified with my next thoughts. *Where were Ma and the baby? Where were Helen and Ardith or little brother, Jamie?* I had to shake off the trembling and fear that kept clutching at my guts. I had to do something. There was just no time for crying.

With hope beating desperately in my heart, I entered the cabin. It was the worst sight that could be imagined. Ma's bloody body was lying amid the debris of little Jenny's crib. With a sob breaking from my throat, I rushed to her side, knowing full well that there was nothing that I could do, yet I had to try to do something that could make things better.

Jumping over the broken furniture, I was quickly at Ma's side. She was torn up and bleeding badly from a vicious beating. Then I could see that she had also been shot. As I bent to tenderly touch her cheek, her eyes flew open, and with a sudden moan, she took a labored breath.

"Momma, Momma!"

"Ah, Matthew," she moaned through broken lips. She clutched at my shirt sleeve with her remaining strength. "He was so vicious! He has as always been this way! Oh, Matt, he took the girls. You've got to find them. Save them from those beasts, please?"

Her eyes wandered over the broken room to where she knew the baby was lying just a few feet away. My eyes followed to where little Jenny lay all broken and lifeless.

"My baby, poor, poor baby! Bring her to me, Matt." That was all Ma could say.

"Shush, Ma, don't try to talk. I'll find them. Just don't talk and waste your strength. I'll go for help, and you'll be fine."

With that said, I staggered over the floor, kicking debris out of my way. I gathered up little Jenny's lifeless body gently into a blanket that lay on the floor and placed her in Ma's arms. There was a bullet hole in Jenny also.

"It's your pa that they were after and some fool map that's supposed to lead them to hidden gold. I told them that if I had a map to where there was gold, Did they think that I would still be here living in this place? But it didn't matter to him who was leading them. He's been a devil since day one."

With a gasp for more breath, she grabbed my shirt and pulled me close.

"Listen, Matt. You must find your pa and warn him. Somehow! Promise me. Find him out West, wherever he is, and warn him. He was headed to Colorado or New Mexico territory after his last visit home. This gang chasing him are worse than animals, and they will stop at nothing until they can get what they want. Your pa will know what to do. He'll know the man who is behind all this. Just tell him it was Mason. That's all he'll need to hear!"

I could barely hear her as she whispered in my ear, "I love you, son. Just you be careful, and never forget what you've learned. Never forget. Be a good man!"

With that said, she took her last breath. Quiet sobs wracked me as I held her body and rocked it back and forth. I knew what she had said, but what was I to do?

I sat there with her head cradled in my lap for what seemed only minutes but what must have been nigh on to an hour. A sound brought me out of his reverie. It was the soft plodding of hooves in the yard that broke the awful silence.

Sorrow had to be lain aside; it was time for action. With a quickness that spurred me on, I searched the cabin for a weapon. The old muzzleloader was still hanging on its pegs over the fireplace. That was what was needed. I knew that it was loaded because Pa always said that an empty gun was a useless tool. With that thought, I pulled it from the pegs and looked down the barrel. The gun and I were ready.

"Hello the cabin!"

Taking the old Hawken down, I stumbled to the door. I was ready to deal with whomever had returned. To my surprise, it was only one man riding one horse and leading another horse with a pack on its back. The two horses looked like twins.

"Boy, you need to be right careful with that there rifle-gun. If it goes off, one of us may get hurt, and I got no hankering to die just yet. Seems like [with a casual glance around the yard] that you could use some help!"

"Light, then," I replied, having made up my mind that he was no threat to me. It just seemed the right thing to do. To trust this stranger after everything else that had happened felt right. I knew that it had been a large group that had done this wreckage. Their boot prints and empty cartridges were everywhere.

"Lordy, boy, what in the hell happened here?"

"I'm not sure."

With that, I proceeded to tell him what little I knew and what Ma had said before she died. Even that wasn't much. Even as I talked with the stranger, he was looking around the yard at all the dead animals, then he looked me over.

What he saw was a tall, young man with sandy-blond hair and greenish-blue eyes. I was at least six foot two or three inches tall and one hundred and sixty or seventy pounds and seventeen years old. He realized that I would be a real load to deal with, even if I was young.

"Boy, have you looked around for anyone else? Would anyone else be alive?"

The question hit me like a slap to the side of the head. Jamie might be lying somewhere, hurt badly.

"I haven't seen my young brother, Jamie!"

"We got to look for him now, son!"

Quickly, I started yelling while walking around. "Jamie, Jamie! Where are you?" In my mind, I was screaming silently, *Please be safe!*

Where in all this carnage could he possibly be alive? I prayed silently that we would find him soon. I just stumbled around the yard between the house and the barn. Then I heard the stranger's voice.

"Hey, boy. Over here. Is this your brother?"

I rushed to see who he had found. It was Jamie, all right. He was lying just inside the barn door, covered in blood. He lay so still that I thought he was dead for sure. The stranger was kneeling beside him, looking to his wounds. It was then that Jamie groaned and began to move his head.

"Steady, young fella. You're in good hands now. Matt, let's get him inside and make sure that he stays among the living rather than joining the dead."

We gently lifted him up and carried him into the house and laid him down on the ripped and torn mattress from Ma and Pa's bed. It was clear that Jamie had been shot at least three times. The worst one was a glancing blow to his head that cut to the bone. Two were bloody but were scarcely more than flesh wounds, nothing life-threatening. But there was a wound to his arm that could be a problem though, since it had sliced through his bicep's muscle. Only time would tell on that one.

"Get my saddlebags, boy, and be quick about it!"

"Sir, can you save him?"

"Well, son, we're shore going to give it our best shot. Get me some water to boiling, pronto!"

With the stranger working on Jamie, I glanced around and began to wander around the house and the yard out front. I had all but forgotten the older girls. In all the searching, there had been nothing left of Ardith or Helen. It was then that I remembered the voice that had ordered them to be taken along and Ma's last words. But to where? More importantly, Why? What in the world did Pa have to do with this? We'd never heard of any gold. If Pa knew anything about gold, I'd never heard of it. We were poor. Gold! Ha! We were low-down poor. But we made by. It just made no sense at all as these thoughts raced through my mind.

Reality has a way of bringing one back to the moment. Rather than stand there with nothing to do, I found the shovel and headed for the old crab apple tree at the back of the house. It was here that the family's small graveyard existed. It was here that an old hired hand that had died of consumption and another baby who was stillborn lay buried. It was here that we would lay Ma and little Jenny to rest.

As the sun slowly sank in the west, I shoveled back the soil and began the grave. With each shovelful of dirt, tears stained the black earth. As each drop fell, I vowed revenge on those who had done this.

"I will find those responsible and bury them into the ground. I promise you, Mom." My tears covered the fresh earth. It was the following morning that we buried her and the baby together.

Time seemed to crawl as we waited for Jamie to mend. It took several weeks before Jamie was well enough to walk without help. During that time, the stranger and I went about trying to piece together the story of that awful day's events. Neighbors up and down the road stopped by and helped with cleaning the cabin. They were the ones who filled in some details. But not by much. Some folks were just trying to help us but couldn't help with any valuable details. Most of what they knew was little compared with what I already knew from Ma's own last words to me.

It seemed odd that after several weeks, I still didn't know the stranger's name, even though he knew mine. All I knew was that without his help, things might have turned out much different for Jamie and me.

I found myself watching the stranger and his beautiful horses from time to time. I hadn't seen horses like these two. They were a pair to be seen. When you put the stranger with the two horses, they all just fit together. The three of them together were a matched set. Both the pack animal and the mare he was riding were twins. Altogether, they were something to see.

It had just been natural to start calling him Mister up to this point. He hadn't been volunteering any information, but he seemed to have a genuine concern for both us boys. He would sit and listen carefully to our cares and worries. He knew the depth of our hurt and applied the only antidote he could offer: time and some understanding.

We all knew that soon Jamie's injuries would require a trip into town.

Chapter 2

The stranger made the decision about Jamie the next day. We got the wagon rigged and headed to town. Along the way, we questioned many of the folks who lived up and down the trace they called a road. No one had seen or heard a thing. The outlaws and our sisters had just up and disappeared.

The stranger and I were talking while the doctor worked on Jamie's arm.

"Where could they have gone to?" I asked.

"Boy, it's a worrisome thing to not know their whereabouts. But as I've learned the hard way, time will bring them to us or us to them. We just got to be real patient. Seems like I heard somewhere that patience is a virtue that we are all lacking. Let's try to take a little time and build up a bit more patience. Eventually, we will find what has been lost!"

"But I'm worried about what might be happening to the girls!"

"Well, Matt boy, jest don't spend too much time worrying over that which you can't change right now. Let's just focus on getting your brother well. Then both of you lads need to be ready to face up to the dangers in this here life and what decisions may lie ahead."

"Listen, mister, I don't need yours or anybody's help. I'm a growed man and can handle what comes my way."

I knew that I shouldn't have said that, but I was just a bit peeved at his thinking that I was not grown-up enough or prepared for life's challenges. His words just rankled me just a bit. I reminded myself that in seven months I would turn eighteen. I would just have to prove him to be wrong.

After some thinking though, I had to admit to myself that he was right. It was hard to accept. It was something that I would never admit out loud. We were just babes in the woods; fair game for the first tough patch to come along. It was a comfort having him there to watch after us, whoever he might be. Me, I had to be a man and fast.

When the doctor was done with Jamie, he called us in to see his work.

"Your brother will be fine in a few more weeks with your help."

"What do we owe you, Doc?"

"Not a dime! Just do what you got to do and be strong! I know what I would be doing if it were me at your ages!"

"Thanks, Doctor, for all you could do! We'll be seeing you."

With that, we headed back to the cabin.

Thinking back, it had been a somber time when we buried Mamma with little Jenny lying at her side. The place I had chosen was on a gentle knoll under the blooming crab apple tree, right next to the other baby. Ma had always admired those blossoms in the spring. On that day, the stranger and I carried Jamie to the grave site where he and I had shed a measure of tears over the grave. We each silently vowed in our hearts that those responsible for these deaths would have justice meted out to them. Someway. Somehow. Somewhere.

While waiting on Jamie to get better, we had cleared up the mess created by the raiders with the help of some of our neighbors. We also repaired the broken front door. Some of the precious windowpanes that Pa had worked so hard to give Ma had to be replaced with shutters. Much of the broken furniture we piled outside to be burned. The bloodstains wouldn't go away, only time would do that.

The month of June came ushering in a long, dry, hot summer. The heat was already like that of July or August. Jamie was mending well, but his right arm would never be quite right. The damage to the nerve and muscle was more than the doctor in nearby Athens could repair. It would require Jamie to relearn everything with his left hand. Eating was one thing he could manage with his damaged right arm but not roping, shooting a handgun, or throwing knives and such since he was born right-handed. These, he would have to relearn with his left hand over time.

Jamie and I were big for our ages and above average in athletic skills. We could thank our Swedish and Irish ancestors for those skills and abilities we possessed. Many a time Dad had reminded us that we were made of Viking blood. Whatever that meant. It was something we would remember as we grew older and some wiser. We just naturally enjoyed running, jumping, climbing, and, yes, even fighting. As brothers went, we were as close as two boys could be. These last two months had drawn us even closer together, and just naturally, we looked out for one another.

Jamie's physical injuries were the least of our worries. The mental turmoil we both carried over the death and the destruction of family and home weighed heavily on our minds. We both knew that it would be some time before either of us would feel any mental healing. It would take time. Jamie and I had started the process to find peace in our lives after all that had happened. Something that we could call normal. The word grief had no meaning to us yet. The word grief always sounded girlish. There were many times, deep inside, we thought we would never get over it. Nights were the worst for us, when the nightmares would explode into our minds with numbing ferocity.

We had taken to sleeping outside under the trees next to the barn. Lying there one night, I was awakened by the sound of sobbing.

"Jamie, you okay?" I could feel Jamie's slight body shake with the sobs that shook through the covers.

"No, I ain't, okay. I miss Ma and the girls, something fierce. Don't you?"

"Yes! But I just refuse to let missing them consume me any longer. Revenge is what is driving me now. I want to punish those who hurt our family!"

That answer was brief but one that allowed me to keep a tight rein on my own emotions. I was trying to be a real tough guy on the outside. It was tough sometimes, even for me. Inside, I was just as torn up as Jamie.

"Listen, Matt. You don't need to act the tough guy with me. I know you feel the same as I do. I know that you just don't want to let anyone know what's eating you."

My only response to him was curt and to the point.

"Try to get some sleep, Jamie!"

Everything that reminded of Ma, the baby, and the girls made my resolve burned deeper into my soul. I had never had these feelings before. Trying to deal with them was even more than I had fathomed.

Wanting revenge on those who had done all this to our family was not enough. I wanted it to be by my hands. Nothing short of their deaths would satisfy the deep hurt that Jamie and I felt deep inside. I vowed then and there that those who had done this foul deed would not go unpunished. For as long as I continued to breath, no one would stop me.

This would be the first and last time that there would be any tears in my eyes and pain in my mind. Not until this journey would reach its end. With that thought, I drifted off to sleep, knowing that with the morning would come another day of life. It would be another day in which Jamie and I could try to get back what had been so violently taken from us: peace, love, safety, and contentment. Revenge had taken that place.

Chapter 3

"Jamie, we've been moping around here long enough. Ma's last words to me were to find Pa and warn him. We also got to find the girls. Me, I think it's time to saddle up and shake the dust of this place."

"Yes, Matt, I know. It's just so hard to cut loose. This here's the only home we've ever had. It's hard to leave it all behind."

It was at that moment that the stranger walked up to join us.

"Boys, if you'll pardon my jumping in here, but I heard in town that ole Smithers has offered to pay a fair price for the place along with the stock animals that are left. Me, I'm for moseying on down the trail. You lads can trail along with me if you want. Mayhap along the way we'll run into someone who has seen the scum who did this terrible ordeal or mayhap hear some mention of your sisters."

I looked to Jamie and he nodded. His reply to the stranger was quick and decisive.

"Let's go see Smithers!"

I straddled the old swaybacked mare to ride the five odd miles into Athens. The stranger had hooked his spare horse to an old cart from behind the barn on which we loaded what few things we intended to take with us. We both knew we weren't ever coming back; that was for sure. The stranger handed Jamie the reins to the wagon.

"It's time, Matt. Lead out!"

Whatever kind of deal Mr. Smithers was apt to make us, we would take. We had no intention of ever returning. There was nothing to keep us, and having nothing was pushing us to leave.

The miles into town went quickly. It was hard to leave the old place and the neighbor folks and all the fond memories. But as I looked ahead, I could see where the road west lay along with the setting sun. Both seemed to draw us on to some unknown destination and fate.

When we arrived in town, the stranger rode his horse down to the barbershop. After tying up the wagon, we trailed behind the stranger as he headed where Mr. Smithers usually spent his time. He was apt to be in front of the merchandise store, spending his time shooting the breeze with the rest of the old-timers who usually spent their time leaned back in the chairs on the boardwalk, chewing on a big wad of chew. Most were whittling on sticks and spitting through the planks. It only took a few minutes of dickering with him to strike a reasonable deal.

Now, all we needed was to see the banker, Henry Foster. Foster was a corpulent yet neat man. His collars were starched and white, seeming to cut into his oversized jowls. The skimpy strings of his lank gray hair lay in perfect slim rows on his otherwise bald head. He was just the kind of man who was disliked by one and all. I guess it was a typical problem for any banker of the time but most of all for Foster. Pa always said that he was a crook and never to trust him.

"What can I do for you, boys?" He stood up behind his desk with his hand out as he spoke to greet us as we entered his office. Once he was settled back in his chair, he commenced to cleaning his fingernails with a small pearl-handled penknife from off his desk. He seemed to act like a king, sitting there behind his oak desk, looking down on us. Jamie and I found seats in front of him.

"We're here to settle up with Mr. Smithers."

Smithers had trailed us into the office, and now Foster could see him there leaning against the doorframe.

"We're selling out to him, lock, stock, and barrel."

The stranger had sidled just to the inside of the door next to Mr. Smithers. He leaned there with his right hand settled on the butt of his holstered gun. He just let his eyes rest on Mr. Foster with a mocking smile. I looked at Foster and could see he was sweating more than necessary that early in the morning. Was that because of the summer heat, or was it the situation of losing something he had wanted and now would never get? Or was it the stranger with his smirk? Either way, Foster was sweating a river as it ran down his jowls and into his shirt collar.

With an effort, Foster pulled himself up to the desk, laying down the knife, and with a hint of a smile, he responded.

"Matt, my boy, it sorrows me to have to point out to you that you aren't old enough to sign legal papers that are required, let alone to be transacting any legal business regarding the land."

He thought he had one on us. But we had the top ace. Jamie and I had anticipated that Foster would try to give us some trouble. He had been eyeing the place for himself. He had even made several visits to see Ma over the last six months trying to persuade her to sell out. Pa had been gone for almost three years when I had just turned fourteen, and Foster knew just how hard things had been for us as a family. But we had come prepared for this fight.

Jamie was standing behind me and just silently upped with the old Hawken rifle. Jamie had carried it in and aimed it in Foster's general direction. He was sitting behind his big oak desk and presented a huge target. Sweat drops sprang from his brow and upper lip as he heard my reply.

My response was just as quick and to the point.

"First off, I ain't your boy. Second, we don't need nor are we asking for any advice from the likes of you." It was hard for me to disguise the contempt that I felt for him.

Foster let his eyes roam around the room. It was when he noticed that Jamie had the old Sharps rifle and it was pointed directly at him.

Jamie was just grinning as he said, "Mr. Foster, I ain't too good at shooting yet with my left hand so you will have to forgive me if I just accidently gutshoot you instead of a heart or head shot. This close, it won't matter to you 'cause you will be dead regardless. You see, we un's don't intend to have any trouble with you on this matter or any other. I suggest that you see how quick you can draw up the papers required, and we'll be on our way. Are you understanding what I am saying?"

Then Jamie pulled the hammer back, which was very loud in the office. The stranger had made sure that the rifle was not loaded, but at that time, Mr. Foster had no idea that it was.

"You boys don't give a man much leeway. No, sirree. None at all!" Foster was trying hard to move this situation along carefully.

"It certainly is our intention. Get on with it, now!" I replied.

With sweat running down his jowls, Foster quickly began to fill out the forms for the sale of the homestead. Mr. Smithers gave Foster the important information concerning the deal we had come to. It was only a matter of minutes and the papers were completed and the signatures were witnessed by one of the tellers and the stranger. I had tried to strain and see what name he signed but it was upside down and too far away to make out.

Old Mister Smithers thanked us as he paid us the money from his own bank account. It was this as much as losing the farm to Smithers that made Foster angry. You could see the anger in his eyes and his demeanor in front of us. It was even harder for Foster, knowing he could do nothing to change things. To lose the money from the bank was surely breaking his cold, hard banker's heart. My thought I kept to myself, but I hoped that Foster could see that Jamie and I just did not have a care about him or his bank.

Through all this, the stranger had not said a word. He just sat back in the background and watched. Nothing ever escaped his notice. His pale-blue eyes never seemed to show any emotion, yet a smile always seemed to lurk just beyond view. He was the kind of man everyone just showed the proper amount of respect. We had noticed that most men usually went out of their way to be polite to him.

More than once did these thoughts come into my brain. *Who was he? What kind of man would let himself get tied to a couple of kids? What made our troubles his? He was a man without a name who we knew and whom we knew next to nothing about. Yet we both knew that on this particular day, it was his presence more than Jamie's rifle that had forced Foster to do what was required and without any trouble.*

With our money in hand, it was time for some decisions. We knew that none of them would be easy.

"Boys, the best I can figure is that we should head west. Maybe first to Murfreesboro and then on to Union City. That's the most likely route that the pack of wolves took who killed your mom and had kidnapped the girls."

"Makes sense. Surely somewhere along the way we will hear something about them!"

"Let's hope so, Jamie."

We headed across the street to the mercantile and bought what provisions we would need along with the rigging. The stranger suggested that we invest in better weapons than the ole smoothbore rifle we had carried from the cabin. The upshot was that we traded for a Navy Colt .36 caliber revolver and a Winchester .44-40 rifle.

We transferred the few possessions we had brought from the cabin, the family Bible, some blankets, a few odds and ends of pots and pans, along with Ma's old cherrywood rocker. There were a few whatnots and such that we placed into a trunk along with the handmade quilts mom had treasured. We hoisted it all into the wagon we had bought. Neither of us knew why, but come hell or high water, that rocker and those few things were going to go west with us. Through it all, the stranger only said what needed and nothing more.

Even after buying all that was needed, we still had over a hundred dollars left over. That was a fortune to us. It was more than Jamie or I needed in our pockets either. Jamie and I had already talked this issue of money over, and we knew what was best for the two of us. I intended to follow through with our decision.

"Mister, we would both like it kindly if you would hang on to this money for us. We will each keep a couple of dollars, and the rest would be best kept by you."

It took a moment or two before he replied to our request.

"I would be honored to do that for the two of you, boys! It's a big thing when you two trust me. Thank you for that trust!"

We had kept out a dollar, which Jamie and I decided to spend on some hard candy. There was still that little bit of a child left in the two of us, so back inside we went. Under the circumstances, we could afford to indulge ourselves this once. We spent more than a few minutes deciding how best to spend our last few pennies.

It was late enough in the day that we decided to spend the night in town and get an early start on the following morning. The best place to bed down was the hayloft of the livery barn. We parked the wagon in the drive lane. It was loaded and ready to roll.

"Matt, you awake?"

"Yes, Jamie. What's bothering you?"

"It's the girls and Pa. You think we'll ever find them?"

"Yes, we'll find them. Just don't you worry none. It may take some time, but remember, that's something we got lots of. Time! Go to sleep now!"

Chapter 4

It became quite a trip. We traveled from Athens to Murfreesboro, then on to Union City. Close to four hundred miles in all. Quite a distance for two boys who had never been more than twenty miles from home. For twenty-six days, we averaged about fifteen miles per day. There were some days that we did more miles and some days less. It all depended on what the stranger had us to learn both from him and the trail.

Jamie and I took turns driving the wagon, one of the easier tasks. But we were learning other things. The stranger was a big help in the learning. He knew things that we would need to know if we were to survive out in the West. We each had to share in the chores, taking turns at building the fire, cooking, tending the horses, and so on.

It was after supper was cleared of an evening that the stranger would begin the lessons of life as he called them. Survival skills were the hardest. Like shooting a gun and hitting what you aimed at, using a knife for defense, reading trail sign, and getting us toughened up physically. The West was a hard environment to be suddenly thrust into, and he wanted us to survive.

"The most important ingredient to survival, boys, is being able to defend yourselves. The best defense usually is to have a better offense than the other guys. Never let the other feller get the top hand. Always be moving. Remember this: guns and other types of weapons are important but not always handy. You have to learn how to use the best weapon the good Lord gave man. Any guess what it is?"

Our silence only urged him on.

"What the Lord gave each of you that he didn't give animals was a brain. Train it and use it occasionally and you will generally always come out on top! One other thing. Never, never trust anyone. You can trust your brother and me but no one else. Remember, I may not be there for you to trust on. Plan to stand alone against whatever trouble that shows up. Do what must be done and then move on. Understand?

"Remember this one thing! The only law where we are going is what you wear on your belt. The gun and the right time to use it is what makes the difference. Know what is right and wrong in your own mind and stand up for the right. Every time."

From that day forward, the stranger began to teach us to use our fists and feet and how to wrestle. He seemed to have a real knack for both, and he bloodied us more than once while doing his "teaching." Further training in the use of knife, hatchet, and bow were done during the evening when the chores were done.

Somewhere along the way, he had learned to knap his own arrowpoints and knife blades, so he passed that knowledge along to us. It took many a day for us to learn how to do this with stone and hammer. He tried to teach us all he knew that would be helpful and necessary for our survival.

He had loosened up once and mentioned the Cherokees concerning certain things he was telling us about. Maybe that was who he learned so much from and that he shared with us, boys. Learning how to track a man or animal was something that we both knew a bit. However, the stranger took what we knew and improved it. He knew that there would come a day when we would need to find the most elusive of game—man. We must know every trick that others would know and then some. We had to learn to improvise if we were to live. All this made us more aware than ever that we did not know who he was. But he certainly knew us.

We were getting closer to the outlaws and the girls with every day. It was in Murfreesboro that we first heard any news of the girls. It was here that things happened that gave the stranger a name besides Mister.

It was a typically warm, clear evening at the end of a very hot July day when we rolled into town. The recent civil war was just three years back. It was still too apparent to not be seen. All we had to do was just look around at the people of the town. Empty sleeves and pant legs identified the survivors of the recent conflict between the States. Some men still had both arms and legs, but they still wore parts of their uniforms or what was left of them.

We were at the edge of civilization. This was where what law there might be was what a man carried in his holster or rifle. Gunfights still happened, and there were still some renegades who would go for a gun to settle even minor disputes that most folks thought no one should die for. Even as we rode into town, there was the sound of guns exploding, and a man fell in the street in front of the saloon, while another man was staggering toward the walkway, blood dribbling down his arm from a wound.

We pulled up to the livery stable. With a few questions, the owner agreed to let us spend the night in the loft. We were unhitching the team when things just started to explode.

Our backs had been to the barn door as we had heard footsteps approaching. The next we knew, the stranger shoved both of us into the dust of the barn.

A single voice called out as we were dropping.

"It's been a long time, Tom!"

It seemed we had barely started falling when the guns were pounding out their deadly rhythm. Jamie and I were both too green to know what to do. So we just lay there. Then silence again filled the air.

"You boys doing all right?" the stranger asked.

"Yeah, we are. How about you?"

"Never better. But I can't say the same for these fellers at the door."

We jumped up to see what had happened, brushing the gritty dirt from our pants, as a crowd of people gathered at the door. What we could see was one man lying face up just inside the door. Very dead. He had been hit three times. The two in his chest could have been covered with a half-dollar, and the last one was centered over his left eye. Another man lay off to the side with no apparent wound until one of the men in the crowd rolled him over. Death had come from a single bullet through the right eye. Each had their guns out and had been fired.

A crowd had quickly gathered around the outside the livery barn. Someone spoke up and asked, "Anyone know either of these jaybirds?'

"You betcha! They was both part of that rowdy crowd that been hanging around Duggan's saloon. They been around town for a week or more. I'd say they are probably just no-count outlaws."

Another old-timer in the crowd looked at the stranger and asked, "Seems that they knew who you were. I thought I heard him call you Tom, right?"

With a wink, the stranger answered. "No, must be a case of mistaken identity. Never saw them before. They just came in yelling and shooting. I don't think they could see good, coming into the dark from such bright sunlight. They took us for someone else. Right, boys?"

There was still just a glimmer of a wink in his eye, and so I spoke up quick, "Yep, whatever they were yelling couldn't be understood. They were just shooting away. Jamie and I would have likely got shot if it weren't for him giving us a shove here."

"Well, don't y'all worry none. We'll see that the sheriff gets all the details and will see to the bodies. Best though that you watch your backs whilst you're in town. There may be more of that bunch what you don't know!" said the same old man sporting a corncob pipe and whiskers to match.

Jamie and I just looked at each other. One thing had just been cleared up for us. Our mystery man's name was Tom. Maybe now he would tell us something about himself. But that subject would have to wait for a more appropriate time.

We quickly walked around the town trying to learn what we could about the gang. Maybe we could find out more about those who had taken our sisters. Many were eager to talk once they learned about our sisters.

Our stay was short because we learned just how close we were to the gang. They had been there only a week earlier.

"Best I can remember was that they said something about heading for Union City," an elderly lady told us.

Then that would be our next stop as well. Perhaps there we could get a better notion of where they were headed or something more of their plans.

Chapter 5

Jamie's arm had healed up nicely, so our evenings were getting more physical. We worked till the sweat ran in streams off our bodies with wrestling, boxing, running, and such. All this work and exercise was hardening up our bodies, replacing baby fat with mature muscles, trained to meet whatever crisis came our way.

Shooting became a contest almost every evening. Shooting a handgun with either hand came easy for me. My large hands and wrists were made for handguns. Jamie, on the other hand, struggled with handguns. However, he excelled at long guns. Give him a rifle, and he could shoot the eye out of a gnat at a hundred yards. We both knew these skills were abilities that would be what would save our lives in the difficult times to come.

There were times when our rough and tumble caused more than just a little blood to flow. Tom was always there to care for it with a dressing and some smooth words to calm the angry tempers that inevitably would explode. Being older and heavier, I gave out more than I received, but on occasion, Jamie would catch me being cocky and nail me with a fist or a new wrestling hold he had just dreamed up.

We were as close as brothers could be, but that summer of tragedy brought us closer together than ever before. We just instinctively came to depend upon one another. If either of us were ever to be in trouble, the other would move heaven and earth to come to the aid of the other.

"Jamie, do you recall those presents Pa sent to us? That must have been after his being home after the war, and then he said he had to head out west."

"Yeah. That must have been less than two years ago. I do remember that he sent a present for each of us!"

"Do you recollect any of those presents?"

"As I recall, there was some dress material for Ma and the girls. A bowie knife for you, a folding knife for me, and things for the baby. Seems like among them baby things, there was a gourd rattle too. Yeah, it was an Indian rattle. Seems I remember that it had designs on the leather that wrapped around the rattle. In the letter Pa had called it an uh… uh… Comanche rattle. I remember that if you shook it, it made noises. What do you think happened to it? I don't recollect ever playing with the darn thing, and baby Jenny never played with it. You reckon it got lost in the raid?"

"I guess not, Jamie! I found it among some of the things Ma had hid away in a special place in the cabin. Remember the old trunk that Pa stashed under the floor boards? Ma had it buried under some old shirts and blankets and such. Seemed like a lot of trouble for a baby's toy. That trunk and everything in it is on the wagon."

It was late that night and time for bed, so the blankets were spread out under the stars. Lying there for a while, waiting for sleep to claim us, Jamie just tossed and turned. He found every little rock and pebble under his blanket that would keep him from sleep. His rolling around kept me from sleeping.

Rising on an elbow, I spoke softly, "Jamie, are you doing all right?"

"No, I ain't! I can't seem to get Ma or the girls out of my mind. My heart aches because Ma is gone. I keep trying to understand it all, but it is still so hard. You know what I mean?"

"Yes, I do, Jamie. Just because I'm older doesn't mean that I miss her any less. More so, that stupid Injun rattle keeps popping into my dreams every night. I just keep remembering the things Ma said at the end. She seemed to have highly treasured that Indian rattle. It was more than just a toy. I remember how she would never let us play with it because it was so fragile. Never did make any sense. None whatsoever."

"Well, how's about you and me settle down and get some sleep. Morning will come early and tomorrow's gonna be a long day. Mayhap, Mr. Tom will tell us about hisself and who he is and why he's in all this."

But we were to learn nothing else for many days to come as we struggled with the daily tasks concerning traveling and camping. Neither of us could forget what lay behind us, nor could we ignore what was in front either. It was necessary to stay on our guard, for we did not know the faces of our enemies yet. It was enough to keep us on edge all the time. But we were ready. We were more than ready.

Chapter 6

If we only knew what was happening with the outlaws and their leader as they tried to outrun us.

"We done stayed too much time back in Murfreesboro! We'll head west. I want things to be taken care, and I mean now! Hear me? See that those who are following us be dealt with. Hear me?"

"Yes, Captain, sir" was all Lane knew to say.

"Hey, Cy, bring those two girls over here. I need to talk to them both and now is as good a time as any!"

Cy walked away and crossed the camp to where the girls were sitting together. They both knew that their lives were in the balance and Mason was the one who could decide their fate.

"Sit down, girls. I have a few questions for you. Don't you be lying to me neither. Understand?"

"First off, where is your father? He has something I want, and I want it sooner than later! Secondly, how long has it been since he was last home, and don't be lying to me, hear?"

Helen answered first without any hesitation.

"As to when Pa left, it was a year and a half ago. Where he was going or why was not shared with any of us. The only one who could have answered your questions was Ma, and you and your gang killed her, baby Jenny, and left Jamie to die."

"What about you, girl?" he asked as he looked at Ardith.

"I have nothing that I could add to what Helen said. Why did you do all this, anyway?"

"Right now, it's not any of your business. What you should keep in mind is that your lives aren't worth a dime to me if you try to sneak away or cause any problems. These men are some of the most dangerous outlaws around. They do my bidding. Do what you're told and cause no trouble and we will all get along. Understand?"

"Cy, take these two back where you can keep an eye on them. Watch Tommy for any nonsense. Understand?"

"Yes, sir."

The gang had spent several days in their camp out of Union City. They had traveled hard and covered many miles since the raid at the cabin. The two girls were smart and knew that any griping about the riding or the food would do them no good. In fact, the two girls spoke right up that first night and said that they would do the cooking, but there was also a big if! That was if they were left alone. Mason knew about each of this bunch too well. They were just the kind of men who would have had their way with the women long before now if he hadn't used a gun and his fists to enforce his rules.

"I need a couple or three to go back to Union City. I expect that Tom killed those idiots we left behind. So, we got Tom and maybe a sheriff's posse following us, and we need to put some time and distance between us and them. Any volunteers?"

"Yes, sir, Captain. The brothers and I will stay. We been looking for a chance to take on brother Tom. Just hurting him a bit is not enough. Not near enough. We have wanted to kill him for a long time. John, Frank, and I will stay behind. It'll be some fun. Right, boys?" The other two nodded for Mason to see.

Mason spoke to himself as he walked away, *I should have known those three were more than ready to take care of Tom. That was why I kept those three around. They are not too smart, but they are all good with six-guns.*

"We have been here long enough. Let's clean up and get the wagon ready. We are heading west, and we are not stopping until well after dark. We'll pull off the road and camp where we won't be seen. I hope you all remember who and what we are after. It is gold and lots of it, and John Allison knows where it is at. Enough to keep most of you in liquor and women for a year or more. We must be on our toes and not let anyone sneak up on us."

With that, Mason turned to the best two of the bunch. That would be Cherokee Lane and Cy Baker. The rest of them were a rag-tag bunch. Two-Trees was a Ponca Indian with a price on his head. Tommy Smith was from New York City, always wore a derby hat, and was a womanizer and killer. James Owen was the cleanest and smartest of the bunch, but he was wanted for killing his own family. Tommy Smith was the one who was wanted in at least three states for rape and murder, and he was a stone-cold killer. Tommy was the one Mason did not trust at all around the girls. The rest were just a ragtag bunch of robbers and thieves who would do anything for a buck. He must also remember that there were several who were relatives of Tom. He was one man Mason hated almost as much as John Allison.

"Cy, just keep an eye on Tommy. Make sure he is nowhere around the two girls. Any problems at all with him, just shoot him where he stands. Put it right between his eyes. The girls are worth more to us if we can use them to get our hands on John and any of the gold. Just don't let those girls out of your sight. I depend on you, Cy and Billy, to ride herd on them two. Understand?"

"Okay, Boss. You got any idea where we might find John or that gold?"

"Well, since we know that the youngest boy lived and that the oldest boy is some shooter from what we hear, we got to consider all that and then add Tom into the equation. We got to go slow but steady. Our best bet is to let Tom and the boys get ahead of us if we can. Then we will just let them lead us to John and the gold. Wouldn't that be grand? When we get the gold then we will kill them all. My guess is that we'll head for the mountains in New Mexico or Colorado and then maybe on south to Mexico. Somewhere like Juarez or somewhere south on the coast. Anywhere away from the states and federal law."

As the fire was dying out, Tommy started in with his Irish songs. He didn't sing well, but it was better than listening to Tobe and his snoring.

"Go change the guards, Lane."

With some time on his hands, he needed to consider the future. Then it came to him what to do the soonest. The next morning it was time to put some of his plan into work.

The idea of sending Tobe and his two brothers back to Union City sounded better and better as the rest of the gang would be heading west. That bunch were just too bloody for even his sensibilities. He should have killed Tobe back at the cabin.

That was also the time when he made up his mind to split the group in to two bunches; one girl in each group. That should make things even harder for Tom and the young boys to find either one of the girls. Yes, that was a great idea. Absolutely!

With that done, he and Lane started the bunch from the campsite to the trail we would travel.

Chapter 7

Perhaps as we headed toward the west there would be a way for us to find out more who Tom really was. For the time being, he would just remain an unknown quantity. He knew all that we needed to survive and then some. Whatever else we needed to know about Tom would happen when he was ready to tell us.

Union City was like so many other cities in the South ravaged by the late war. Faded uniforms with missing legs and arms were mute evidence of men who had given the full measure expected. Pain and anger were etched in their eyes and faces. There were lines drawn by hunger, thirst, and unimaginable suffering. Many had had their courage drained away on distant battlefields and had obviously found a new type of courage in a bottle of rye whiskey or 'shine. Nothing we had seen before this had prepared us for the sights of Union City.

As we entered the town, everyone's eyes seemed to be on us. They were probably trying to figure out where we were from. They knew we were from the East and guessed as much because we were headed west. They knew that anyone in their right mind did not want to be there today or any other day.

Most folks took note of our weapons and such, but they always seemed to linger over Tom just a shade longer than the rest of us. There was something about his manner that drew people's eyes. Later on, I would understand. The fact was, and is, that without him, we would have died. For now I just was more than glad he was with us. It was just a part of his nature to try to avoid trouble when possible. Yet we all knew that sometimes it was unavoidable. What couldn't be avoided was the trouble that seemed to be riding with us. I could see that Tom wished to keep us from all that he could.

"Boys, I'm going into the mercantile for some supplies and some conversation. Take the rig down to the livery and get that broken tongue fixed right. Also, remember that the offside mule needs to be reshod. I'll find you later at the livery."

I noticed that Tom's eyes had not moved off the store and people inside as he had been talking and as he tied his horse to the rail.

We stood still while he started walking into the store. Jamie still sat on the wagon seat, and I was standing in the street not really knowing just what to do. I knew that we should do as Tom had told us, but I had a notion that trouble was in the wind. I was starting to learn how to listen to this kind of wind and know which the direction it was blowing.

I continued to watch Tom as he paused at the edge of the street next to his horse. He brushed the dust off from his pants and boots with his felt hat and patted his gun. He already had the thong off his gun.

Jamie and I knew just what the folks were seeing. Tom was a tall, lean horseman with no fat on his work-hardened frame. Most people would have said that he was skinny, but there was immense hidden strength in his arms and legs. His face was the kind that most women considered as handsome. Like most horsemen, his legs were bowed from years in the saddle and were laid with muscles like iron. It wasn't the clothes nor was it the guns that drew people's attention. It was the man.

It was all those things that make a man. It was that and more when rolled into a package that people admired along with those intangibles that make a person want to look twice, particularly women. All the years he had spent on the trail with its hardships had forged the steel of his life into a keen, sharp edge.

Before doing anything else, Tom eased the loop off his pistol and eased it in and out of the holster a time or two. That was all I needed to see that he would need some help. Tom again silently swiped the dust from his pants with his hat while letting his eyes roam up and down the street. He noticed the people walking and lounging on the boardwalks. Nothing missed his gaze. Tom looked back at Jamie and I and spoke clearly.

"You boys get down to the livery. I'll see you later."

"Tom, you need a hand with anything?" I could sense the smell of trouble in the air. I knew that he needed me whether he wanted to say so or not.

"No, Matt. I'll handle whatever pops up!"

Even as Tom was walking away, I told Jamie what I was going to do.

"You go ahead, Jamie. I'm going to help whether he knows it or not."

With that, I gave Jamie that look, and he knew what I meant. Trouble was right there, and I was going to deal myself in, if for no other reason than to help Tom.

Jamie had only moved a short way down the street when I saw the hesitation in Tom's stride. Tom took time to pull his handgun up and down twice to make sure it was ready for work. Whatever was riding Tom was sending a chill running up and down my spine. Something was wrong, but for who and why? I could feel trouble in the air like a cold hand resting on my shoulder.

"You be careful, Matt." Jamie called as he and the wagon went down the street.

I had grabbed up the carbine when I jumped from the wagon to the street. Haste had seemed to be the order as I had sprinted back to the mercantile not knowing what to expect. I got there just in time to catch the door as it was swinging shut. I was not to be disappointed.

Before I went in, two old-timers stood at the door, looking in, as I was holding the door from closing.

"Boy, you best don't go in thar! It's sure trouble that your pard is a facing."

"Maybe he might need someone to watch his backside, don't you reckon?"

"Well, youngster, it'll be your funeral!"

The scene inside was tense. Tom stood stiff-legged by the pot-bellied stove across the room from the door. It was not one but three hard cases who were bracing him from across the store. With that quick glance, I knew that I had made a right choice in coming to help him. There were several customers who had stepped as far as they could from where the shooting was going to happen. The store owner had just dropped to the floor behind the counter.

Everyone could clearly hear the words being exchanged by Tom and those who had been waiting for him.

"We seen ya ride in with John's brats, Tom. We surely did think we had cleaned out his nest. Why should you be making this your trouble anyways? I thought for sure that you would stay out of this, being we are family and all. You know that the last time we met we made you a promise. Now it's that day. You're going to die regardless. You have interfered with our business for the last time! Now it is as good time as any to pay up!"

The speaker was the most disreputable character of the three. He was so dirty and unkempt as any person could be. You could smell the foul odor from where I was standing. This fella was dressed as a dirt farmer, overalls and all, except for the gun hanging on a huge belt around his middle. He really liked to hear himself talking.

Tom took a deep breath and did some talking himself.

"I guess your mind is all clouded up. It was the major and his wife who were my friends. Have been for as long as I can remember. When everyone else had deserted me and left me for dead, they were the ones who took me in and nursed me back to life. If they had not been there, I would have died. You of all people should remember that, Tobe! What I want to know is, what was in that cabin that was so valuable that you would have killed his wife and child and leave the one boy for dead? She was too good a woman to die like that. And the baby, Tobe! A baby, and she was only three years old. It was not necessary at all. You all should die for that killing alone. Taking the girls as prisoners was the last straw!"

"Well, Tom, since you ain't leaving here alive, I surmise I can tell ya the truth of things. It were fer some type of fool Injun rattle and lots of gold. Can you believe that?"

It was with a sly glance at his partners that he smiled as he finally said, "Well, this talk has gone long enough. It's too bad you had to interfere. You should have taken a different direction. You seemed to be a little pale. Maybe sick to the gullet, and the medicine fer today will be lead pills administered in bullet size." He was laughing at his own sick joke.

I decided it was my turn to pull some cards in the game so to speak, so I spoke out aloud for Tom to hear.

"You go right ahead and kill those two, Tom."

It was a grim smile that crossed Tom's face when he heard me.

"Me, I got the farmer on the right here all staked out for my own self." This one had seen me as I stepped into the room. He was wearing striped overalls with only one strap and a gun butt hanging from his front pocket and run-down old farmer's boots.

"All right, Tobe, you've called it!"

With that, Tom's guns leapt from his holster and the one behind his belt like magic. Even with everything going on, my one thought was that someday I wanted to be as fast as Tom with a handgun.

With Tom's words, the room erupted with exploding guns. Smoke billowed out the door and windows, obscuring the view of the room. I could hear a loud groan and then a thud as a body fell to the floor. I hadn't even been aware that I had fired, but the evidence lay across the room where the farmer in striped pants lay in a slowly spreading pool of blood. One of my shots had hit him in the upper arm and nearly tore it plumb off. The other had taken a chuck of skin from his left hip.

In just a few seconds, the smoke had begun to clear from the room. The crowd that had gathered behind me could see what I could see. The best I could see was that there were three who were either dead or badly wounded. They were lying around the front of the store counter. The one called Tobe was dead from several wounds, but the one that killed him was the ugly throat wound. The other man would never see this world through either of his natural eyes. Tom's aim had been rock steady even as they were shooting at him. Tobe, apparently, was the one who had come the closest to killing Tom.

As I stepped farther into the store, I could see Tom up close. I could see that he had at least a graze on his left arm, but the one that hurt the most was on his left side, down low. With a groan, Tom just let go and slid down the wall onto the floor. I was close enough for me to try to help him up. But I could see that he was needing a doctor as he was bleeding from his side and his left arm.

"Tom, what should I do? You can't go and die on us, you know. Jamie and I need you!"

"Matt, that's the nicest thing that you ever did say. Also, a bit stupid. Yes, I'm hurt but not so bad that if you get some help over here and get me to the doc, he could put a plug in this hole in my side before I bleed out totally." With that said, he just passed out cold.

It was the two same old-timers who had followed me in that came to lend me a hand.

"Here, boy. Let's give you a hand with Tom. He's gonna need the doctor right soon."

The two old-timers quickly put crude bandages over his wounds and bound them in place. By that point, several had stepped into the store, so with their help, they got Tom on an old door and proceeded to carry him to the doc's office.

Halfway across the street, Tom stirred back awake. It was the touch of one of the old-timers who then asked, "You all right, boy?"

Tom's rough response was just as quick.

"You betcha! Iffen you old boys don't drop me on my head here in the street. I'll be all right if Doc can sew me without a lecture again!"

As they gently laid him on the table in the doc's office, Tom turned to see me standing there. "Thanks, Matt. You did just fine back there. Mind you, keep the bears off the doc's back while he patches me up. Know what I mean?"

"Don't you worry, Tom. I got it covered!"

I took a seat right outside the door, watching all that was going on, and I could see Jamie busy with the wagon. I was surprised that the folks around us knew him and most of them were all voicing their concern for Tom's well-being. I was full of curiosity. Perhaps as I sat here, I could learn more. I could see the doctor running down the street to his office.

"Heh, Doc. Get in here. You got a patient who needs your professional care. This here's young Tom, back again!" said the same old-timer from the store.

"Well, well. It is our boy, Tom," the doc said as he wiped his hands clean. "Looks like you haven't lost your old habit of showing up here and needing some patching or mending. One of these days you're gonna get a terminal case of lead poisoning if you ain't more careful."

Tom was awake again. "Listen, Doc. Can't you just patch me up and leave off the sermonizing? I got these two young boys with me, and we got a long way to go, and we got things to get done!"

With the doctor working on him, Tom let out a screech that could be heard all the way to the next county and passed out again.

After about ten minutes, the doctor was just finishing the work on the shoulder wound when Tom woke up again.

"Hello, Tom. Glad you are awake now. Some of the fellows have already seen to them yahoos over in the store. Frank Clayton was the one the boy shot, and he will more than lose his arm, if he don't go and die completely."

Another old-timer spoke up from the door, "Frank just died! Ole Tobe was good and dead before he hit the floor along with the other brother, John Riles."

Tom had heard those words and replied to them.

"I just put my shots where they'll do the most good for bad men like them. I've never felt any kindness toward any of them. Not at all! They had none for me, that's for sure!"

The one old-timer just kept own talking. "I never could understand Tobe. He just wasn't worth much. He wasn't good from the start. He and John started to steal before they was even ten years old. Was it true what you said about Tobe, John, and the others. Did they really kill a woman and her baby?"

"Yes! That young man who helped me was Matt. His brother, Jamie, was the one driving the wagon. It was their mother and baby sister, Jenny, who were killed in Tennessee. It was their older sisters, Helen and Ardith, who were kidnapped."

"Well, I guess them yahoos got what they had coming. We can see how you never felt any brotherly love to any of that bunch. For them to do what they did was just too much."

For me, this was a revelation and a half. I could now understand that Tom had just shot his half brothers to death. He did it without any feelings whatsoever. So he had several half brothers. Getting to know Tom was getting deeper and more interesting every day that we spent with him.

The doctor had finally removed the bullet and was ready to put a bandage on the wound. After looking over the shelves, he found just what he wanted. He said that if he used it on the wound, it would help it in healing. Before Tom could complain, Doc poured the solution from the jar on his shoulder and then his hip wound. That got Tom yelling so loud that he could be heard across the town.

"God almighty, Doc! That was liquid fire. It was turpentine, wasn't it?"

"I believe so, son. Better for some of the cure than a shoulder full of infection that will still kill you. Just you lie there whilst I put a bandage on without any more noise from you."

Tom's eyes scanned the room until he made contact with mine.

"Come here, Matt. I got to thank you proper for saving my life, boy." With that, he took my hand in his own and held it for a moment.

"See here, you don't seem none too upset. That's the first man you ever killed?"

"I guess I'm not, Tom. The man you called Tobe said that they were there at the cabin when Ma and little Jenny were killed. It seemed that they needed to die for treating our family that way. To me it was not different than shooting down a rabid dog or skunk. It just needed doing."

"Well, you got to be feeling something, don't you? You can't just shoot a man down and not have some emotions?"

I walked away without an answer, just a brief stare for them all. Tom reflected on that stare for a few moments. Tom could actually feel some of the fear that the others would feel if and when they ever have to face me. Fear was something that I wanted our enemies to feel. There would never be any tears for these killers.

Tom could read me like a book. He had read this book before. It was just too familiar. All he could think was for himself.

"Time, boy. Give it time!"

I knew that Jamie would be fretting himself, wondering what had happened. My thoughts quickly turned to him and the other immediate things that needed doing. So I quickly turned to Tom.

"Tom, I got to help Jamie. He'll be wondering what happened to you and all."

"Hang on a minute, Matt. Just hold up there, would ya?"

Even though it hurt, he dug down in his pants pocket and came up with two double eagles.

"Make sure that the wagon gets fixed and then load up the provisions we talked about. You can get them at the mercantile. You and Jamie get yourselves a bite to eat and then come back by here with my horse and the wagon. We got to be moving on."

"Whoa up there, Tom. You can't leave here! You're bad hurt. You're gonna need some tending to."

"Well, Doc, these boys can do for me as much as you can and a bit more gentle. No offense, Doc. Besides, we got to get on down the trail. We believe their sisters are very close. We must keep going. We need to put some heat on the gang, and they know we're on their trail.

It was two hours later before Jamie and I got back to the doc's place. The doctor was still arguing with Tom when Jamie and I loaded him up.

"You boys pay attention and follow my directions in taking care of his wounds. Don't let any of his yammering bother you. He will heal up well if you listen and do things as I told you. Hear?"

Doc could see that we were leaving so he gave us some final instructions on how to care for Tom's wound along with a tin of salve to assist the healing. He was guessing that before things were done that us boys would need some of his salve.

Jamie and I made sure the doc knew we had heard him clear. With that, we headed off down the road. We had fixed a bed in the middle of the wagon bed as comfortable as we could. As we pulled out with the late afternoon sun in our eyes, we could still hear old Doc Winters as he was fussing and fuming to anyone who would listen.

"He's a damn fool for going off like this. But he's our fool, by God! Good luck to ye boy and those younguns too."

There was one more amazing thing that happened as we left the town.

An old, ragged man rushed out to stop us. He got close, waving his hands in the air. Jamie and I sure didn't know who he was, but Tom quite obviously did. The old man got close enough and leaned over the side of the wagon. He smelled like a saloon, of smoke and booze, as he spoke quietly to Tom.

"Are you all right, son?"

"Yes, sir, I'm alive!" was Tom's simple reply.

"I heard ye was in town. I also knew that those low-life boys would be trying to sand you down. I figured that there was nothing that you couldn't handle as it appears. You understand about why I could not interfere, don't you, boy?"

"Sure, you just rightly couldn't stand by and see me gunned down by your other sons. Like so many other things, you would have grieved for me all of two seconds, just like the three who are lying dead. Doesn't look like you have shed any tears for those three. Another drink for you and all else will be forgotten. Don't even try to tell me you took to caring for me just all of a sudden. The only person you care about is your own self."

The silence that followed seemed painful. Tom knew that we were wondering about this bittersweet reunion.

Finally, the old man said, "Son, ain't you gonna ever forgive me after this long a time?"

"Forgive you? Yes. Did that a long time ago. Forget? Not in your or my lifetime. That, I will never do, Pa. I will not forget. Maybe some time far in the future. Just don't push it with me. Hopefully, I'll see you again sometime and we can talk about some of those things! Maybe if you could stop the drinking, that would be the first step toward sanity on your part!"

The old man turned and stumbled away toward the side of the road. His mumbling words were clear to all our ears.

"Time, boy. That's something I ain't got much of," he said as he stumbled off toward an old lean-to house there at the edge of the town. Even as the old man waved goodbye, he already had a bottle in his hand.

This was such an amazing happening for Jamie and me. Tom, up to this time, had tried to keep many of the details of his life from us, and now here we were, meeting and killing his half brothers as well as meeting his father, such as he was. The old-timers in this town sounded more like his father than this drunk. This was a new revelation. Why did he forgive him? For what? It was sure a mystery to us.

Chapter 8

"Get this rig moving, boys," he said as he lay back down in the wagon.

"Time's a wasting. We got to get to New Madrid as soon as we can!"

With that we left the town far behind us as we headed west on the trail. We knew that Mason's gang were trying their best to stop us or hide from us without much luck. Our direction, just like the gangs, was northwest toward the crossing below where the Ohio river enters the Mississippi. Tom said that was the easiest crossing for many, many a mile.

It was hard to imagine just how Tom must have suffered on that trail ride. But it wasn't in him to complain. Often a groan would escape his lips, which he would cut off just as quickly as it came out. He didn't want us to worry about him at all.

We went several days without either of us mentioning his father or the events back behind us. We just made sure he had a canteen full of cold water and some shade from the sun.

On the fourth day, Tom finally spoke up from the wagon bed as we moved down the trail.

"Boys, I heard that the wild bunch that has your sisters should be on the west side of the river around New Madrid. That's why Tobe and the others were left behind to deal with us. They wanted to slow us down or stop us. That's why we have to be careful like. Mason and his thugs will take no time at all to rape and kill the girls. They are trying their best to stay ahead of us, so we will do nothing that they can hear about us. It's going to take two or three days for me to heal up, and then we can try to tackle them again."

That was when we learned the name of the leader of the gang. Mason! Who was he, and why so much hatred?

Instead of a half day to get to the river, it was late in the evening two days later that we stood near the bluffs overlooking the Mississippi. A low fog covered the river bottom not letting us see very far ahead. It was a good time to pull up to give the mules a blow. On the lee side of a bluff, we found grass and a spring surrounded by new growth trees. When we asked Tom about the sparse growth, he replied that it was the result of a fire set by troops from one side or the other early in the first year of the war. The trees and grass had grown back in eight years of quietness.

Jamie got down and had a brisk fire burning so that coffee would be ready for us all. I helped Tom out of the wagon and propped him against a small boulder close to the fire. It only took a few minutes to slice strips of bacon into the pan, then he fetched out the loaf of bread, which he sliced up generously for us. Eggs would have been great, but they just weren't to be had along the trail. But it was a meal that would stay with a person until the next one rolled around.

Once the meal was over, time was spent talking about the past three or four days. Finally, Jamie and I hoped that Tom would decide that this was the time to fill in the details about his family and such that pertain to our little journey. But not this time. Not a word was said as we lay down for the night.

The next morning sun burned the early fog away and showed the way west. It sure was a sight to behold. The majestic Mississippi River. It was all of a mile wide and rushing by like a freight train bound for the Gulf of Mexico. Big saugers, uprooted trees, were rolling in and out of the water. These big trees with their massive roots were always a threat to rip the bottom out of a boat or raft while going down or across the river.

Since there was no breeze, the surface was dimpled with little waves and peaks. We rolled the wagon down to the landing where we waited for the ferry. The ferry was nothing more than a big wooden raft, big enough for the wagons, mules, Tom's horses and us. A strong cable had been stretched across the river, allowing the raft to move across. The owner, who was the pilot, kept his eyes on the river and the wind while moving us and the load safely to the other side. Jamie and I were awed by the sight of the river and that we would be able to move across without any incidence.

The ferryman was an acquaintance of Tom's, which made us feel a certain amount of comfort. But not much.

"How do, boys. Where do ye be bound?"

"West." We echoed.

The mules were not inclined to climb on to the raft, but we finally convinced them to join Jamie and the horses and the few other folks who were on the raft with the pilot's help.

The pilot had given his directions that would work on both sides. "Just ease up on the reins, and I'll lead them on now and off fer ye on the other side."

It was when he was leading Tom's horses that he commented, "Heh, now isn't this young Tom's favorite horses?"

"Yeh, they are his horses. He's here in the back of the wagon. He's just a little under the weather!"

"Well, boy," he said to Tom as he leaned over the back of the wagon, "what seems to be ailing you?"

"Hello, Mr. Morgan. It's just some pain in the shoulder and top of my hip. Too much lead I picked up down the trail. I was fairly lucky."

"And just what kind of shape did ye leave those who provided the lead?"

"Let's just say that they're not suffering anymore."

"I can just guess who it were that tried to put you out of commission. It were that no account half brothers of yourn, Tobe and those other two. I had heard tell that Tobe volunteered to stay behind and the other two were right behind him in volunteering. Tobe was all fired up to put you down so's the rest of the gang could keep on going out west."

"You guessed right. Sounds like you met the whole bunch?"

"Yes! You'd be guessing right. Those three went back east after a day or two in Madrid!"

"Yes. I killed Tobe and John. That young man, Matt, there took care of Frank!"

"Well, the rest of them are at least a day and a half ahead of you. You just ride real careful around that bunch. They are not to be trusted, ever. They tried to run over me without paying for passage. But me and my twelve-gauge shotgun learned them to behave and pay before they even got on my raft. I reminded the whole group of what folks on both sides of the river would do to them. If they were to kill me, there are those who would trail them to the ends of the earth to deliver punishment. No one rides over the river for free, but folks pay me because they are as safe when they are on my raft as anywhere."

"Well, I'm guessing that there must be only eight of them left, not counting the two young ladies. But you be careful. I heard Mason talking to Cy Baker, and he wants him to find some more men to do a special job! That was all I could hear without looking nosey. You know what I mean! Them kind think old folks are hard of hearing," he said as he chuckled.

"Those young women were our sisters. How were they doing?"

"Well, young man, they seemed fine at that time. But watch real close with that bunch. They will kill ya for a nickel in your pocket. When you finally run down this bunch, just shoot straight and bury them deep. That bunch surely do deserve it. Yes, they do!"

Chapter 9

It was a week later before we arrived at New Madrid. As towns went, New Madrid was as sorry as they come. It was really nothing more than a collection of cabins that sat above the ground on pilings. It got Jamie and me wondering why they were built that way, so Jaime asked Tom the why of it.

"Well, Jamie. They're that way so's they can be moved real quick like! You see, the river yonder has a way of eating away at the bank. That's the reason they have to keep moving the houses and such back a little further each time it floods."

I wondered out aloud myself, "Seems like a lot of trouble. I'd just find me a better place to live, far from the river and the flooding!"

"That's easy for you to say, Matt. You're only passing through. Some of these folks have lived all their lives here. The river and the land are their very lives."

Tom continued to fill what he knew about the town. New Madrid's one main street was rutted by the wagons used to haul mostly poor-grade cotton down to a deep water landing on the river. Since the end of the war, steamboats were used more to travel up and down the river besides carrying cargo. That was why the folks of Madrid built the pier as a likely stopping place. It was here that riverboats could buy food stuff for folks riding the boat and could see what was available to haul on down the river. Those folks who were lucky enough to have any crops to sell were getting good prices since the passengers liked to eat well.

Among the tar paper and board buildings, we found the local mercantile store. From the outside it appeared to be ready to collapse, but inside, it was crammed with every conceivable item a person could need. There was food of all kinds, clothes, and tools of every kind. There was even some furniture. Most items were castoffs from travelers looking to lighten their wagon as they headed west.

And oh, yes, there were shoes, boots, and guns! Jamie and I had never seen that many firearms in one store ever. Jamie was more interested in the sugar candy, while I was looking at a new pair of boots and looking over again and again at what sidearms there were to be had.

Tom had taken his time in getting down from the wagon and had walked carefully into the store. He finally got the attention of the proprietor and commenced to order what we needed to continue our journey west. While he busied himself, I hunkered down by a rack of boots where I could size them up. I was needful of a good pair of boots as was Jamie. Where my thoughts were about my feet, Jamie was thinking of his sweet tooth.

"Here, Matt. Try these on," he said as he handed me a pair of woolen socks and a pair of tough cowhide riding boots.

"Maybe this pair will fit those big feet of yours. Be sure that there is ample room for some more growth in them."

Tom's eye was pretty good for sizing and the boots did fit. I knew I'd get blisters breaking them in, but I wouldn't mind. I'd never had a new pair of boots like these before. The brogans that I pulled off were so done for. Once they were off, I threw them into a trash barrel.

Tom had finally collared Jamie and was trying to find him a pair of boots that were small enough for his feet. Jamie was big but his feet just never kept up with the rest of him. He had to settle for a pair of brogans. At least these brogans were tough and should last him for a while. Next followed some homespun pants for both of us. We bought the pants long in the leg to allow for some growing. Me, I just poked the extra part down in my boots as I had seen Tom and others do. A couple of homespun cotton shirts came next, and then gloves and coats completed our outfits.

The clerk was loading up our goods while we had continued to shop. We were headed for the door when I noticed Tom was just standing there. I hesitated at the door to see what he wanted or what was on his mind. Then he spoke his mind.

"Whoa up there, boys! There is one last thing we needs to do. Matt, you're lacking one essential tool that every young man at your age on the frontier needs. Your own handgun. You boys have learned well how to use my weapons and the spare we bought back in Athens, but you need your own ones."

The clerk had heard our conversation, so he chimed right in. "Gentlemen, we have a fine stock of both used and new weapons. If you will step back to the back counter, I would be glad to show you our inventory."

"I think I'm going to need some help making my choices, Tom. How's about some help?"

Tom had seen what I had been looking at, so he knew what was needed.

"It would be my pleasure, Matt!" It was times like this when Tom sounded real educated.

Tom looked over the guns stacked on the shelves and hanging on the wall. Some were in holsters, others lay naked collecting dust. There was every size and shape imaginable. Finally, Tom asked for one in a holster with a cartridge belt wrapped around it. The holster and belt were enough to get anyone's attention. Someone had spent some time and detail in carving a small acorn and leaf pattern in the belt and holster.

Tom lifted the gun out of the holster and looked it over carefully. He worked the cylinder and hammer a few times, then broke it down and glanced down the barrel. Then he handed it to me for my inspection. It was then that I noticed that the barrel had been shortened and some very fine smithwork had been done to make the balance just right.

The clerk noticed my questioning look. "It belonged to a feller who thought he was a gunfighter."

"Well, how is it you've got his gun?"

"He's got no use for it now. He wasn't near as fast as he thought he was. Even if he had practiced more, it would not have helped in the end!"

I just continued to examine the gun. Its balance and feel felt perfect. It seemed like it was made just for me. According to Tom, this was something that every shooter should do before buying any type of firearm. Then I handed it back to Tom with a nod.

"It'll do, Tom."

"Do you have any cartridges handy?" Tom asked the clerk.

"Sure nuf, just help yerself." With that, he put a box of shells on the counter.

I watched Tom as he loaded the pistol. Then he nodded at me as he led us both out the back door.

"What's up, Tom?"

"Never buy a handgun or rifle unless you can try it out." With that in mind, he handed me the gun.

"How does she feel to you being loaded?"

For me, I can still feel the tingle I felt the first time when my hand closed on the walnut grips. The balance was perfect. It seemed to have been made for my hand. My eyes revealed what my hand was telling me of the careful craftsmanship and detail that it had taken to make such a fine weapon. It never came from the factory this good.

We stepped out the back door, and I saw the old stump about thirty feet away. Others had used the stump as a target, and it would work for me. I was still holding my arm and the gun against my right hip. As I took a second step to land on the ground, Tom was ready for me.

"Shoot now!" was all he said.

In less than a heartbeat, I raised my eyes to the target and the gun responded without a pause. Five shots rolled out as one. The sounds seemed to reverberate like a small cannon. When the smoke cleared, we both walked out to see the damage. It was easy to see that the five shots were placed so that a man's hand could have covered all of them. Tom bent over to examine the pattern.

"Not bad, Matt. That's a real good group. How's does it feel to you?"

"Well, by the last shot, she was pulling high and some to the right. Other than that, it felt really good."

"You've got a good eye, Matt. Howsomever, it wasn't the gun's fault. It was in your hand and grip. That's something we can work on. A little exercise will build up your grip. Well, let's see what this money gouger wants for it."

The clerk informed us that we would have to dicker with the owner of the store on this one. We got back in the store just as the owner came walking toward us.

"Well, Mort, how much?"

"My word, it is you, Tom, in the flesh! The report was that you had been killed or injured severely!"

"Well, Mort, I'm glad to see you too. Obviously, I am still alive. I just got scratched a bit. Now, how much for this gun for Matthew?"

"Well, actually, Tom, it's yours already!"

"How's that?"

"The previous owner is buried up on the knoll. His last wish was that if I was to see you, you were to get his gun, his horse, and the rest of his gear. He must have been a friend of yours? He died without any time to explain by all that."

Tom's eyes opened even wider as he looked over the gun. He twisted it around in his hands. As his fingers trailed over the wood grain of the butt, the realization came to him of who the owner had been. This he verified by finding the initials, GC, engraved on the butt strap.

"No, Mort. Gilbert Cole and I were friends once upon a time. Then things changed, and his anger got the better of him. We had a real knockdown fist disagreement and I won. But as I rode away, he swore to kill me the first chance he got. We had become enemies, and yet we still respected one another. Given time I think he would have gotten over the whole issue. But with him, it was a matter of family and pride. He should have stayed back home. Maybe he did get over, and that was why he was here."

"Who was it that killed him, Mort?"

"It was that no-account half brother of yours, Tobe, along with John and Frank. They were the ones left behind by the gang to watch for you and the younkers. Gilbert, the gun's owner, had heard them talking of how they were going to kill you if you made it this far. He knew these fella's planned to deprive him of his own revenge. So, he up's and challenged them in the street. I think he might have had a chance if he would have gone for his gun right then without waiting. But Tobe and the other two never batted an eye. They just pulled and drilled him before he could draw his own gun. He had no chance at all! He died awful hard. It took almost a full hour before he died. That was when he gave us his last will, so to speak. His last words were for you, Tom. He said he forgave you and hoped for the same thing from you. Said you was the closest to him like a brother."

Tom's face was a mask that couldn't be read. But the tone of his voice couldn't blunt his emotions.

"Those three have finally reached their reward. They all died, and thank God for that. That's three less we have to face down the road."

"Good for you!" was all Mort could reply.

"By the by, the horse and other gear are at the horse corral. Maynard can give you what Gilbert said about the horse and all. Good luck!"

With a glance at the sun to see the time, we collected Jamie and headed out of town. Me, I stood just a little bit taller after strapping on the gun.

"I think that Gilbert would be proud to know that you'll be using his weapons and horse, Matt. Right proud!"

"Well, I guess that I will do my best to use the guns properly on those who need it most!"

On the way out of town we stopped at the livery barn to get the horse and gear. That was a surprise too. This man, Gilbert, he knew horses. The lineback dun Appaloosa that the hostler brought out showed a mixture of the best that could be found. He had all the graceful lines to appease the eye, and yet he appeared strong through the chest to stay the distance. He was for sure no prima donna. He was a man's horse, all sixteen hands of uncut stallion. He appeared at the stable door, dragging the hostler with every step.

I was already down from the wagon and reaching for the lead rope before I even realized what I was doing. The stallion was rearing and trumpeting, but I quickly grabbed the rope next to his halter and he immediately settled down. He took a quick blow at my face and smelled me, and I knew I was in love with him. I spoke gently in his ear and stroked his neck to keep him calmed even more. I knew then that the stallion's name had to be Duke.

"You look to have the right touch, Matt!"

"Be careful, Matt" was all Jamie could say. Jamie was ready to see me being thrown around by the biggest horse that either of us had ever seen.

The livery owner said, "Son, this horse is as ornery as I've ever seen in all my born days. I'll be glad to be rid of him. Since his owner up and got killed, he has been downright dangerous. Nothing and nobody has been safe around him. Mares, geldings, or any person. I swear the truth!"

"What do we owe you for his keep, ole-timer?"

"Nary a dime, Tom. That Gilbert feller done paid up before he got hisself killed. It weren't more than a week or so back. I 'spect you done fer Tobe and his brothers since you are still here and breathing and they are not."

"I can see that your eyesight is still sharp as an eagle, Maynard. Yes, it was Tobe, Frank, and John who we met back over the river. Isaiah is somewhere ahead of us. But his time will come, I'm sure. Is there some gear with this hoss?"

"Yeh, it's jest inside the door. Help yerself!"

While they had been talking, I had tied the stallion to the end-gate of the wagon while Jamie hustled in and helped bring all the gear to the wagon. The saddle and bridle were a matched set with just enough silver mounting to be appealing and yet not too showy. An Indian blanket and saddlebags completed the outfit with a tooled saddle.

"Well, Matt, this is your day. Not only do you get your first real sidearm but your very own hoss and gear to boot. Gilbert would be pleased for you to have them, I'm sure. Make sure that you got that stud tied tight. Throw that blanket over the gear in the wagon and let's be on our way."

The hostler started to gimp back out to us as we headed for the wagon. "Hold up now. Just hold up! This here Winchester goes with the gear. You don't want that scabbard to be empty. Go easy as you go, Tom. Don't give those wild outlaws any leeway whatsoever."

With that we headed west to a fate which was still unknown and as yet to be determined. I knew that from that moment forward this journey would be even more difficult for us all. As I thought of it, I knew that there was going to be more pain, death, and destruction than we had seen so far. But I knew we had to do it. Hopefully, not our pain or death!

Considering all this, Tom was not totally healed from his wounds. I was trying to keep the anger and resentment from building up inside me. Who knew what Jamie was feeling also. Jamie was like me in that respect that he very rarely talked about his feelings. It had been close to six months since the gang who raided our home, killed our mother and baby sister and stolen our two older sisters. Each mile we traveled got us that much closer to saving them. Maybe we would feel better once we were rid of the revenge that had filled our hearts and souls.

Chapter 10

We were eager to leave New Madrid and head west toward Springfield. There were many small villages and towns we passed through as we crossed southern Missouri. We took our time, but there were no more ambushes or gunfights to deal with.

We were getting closer to finding Mason and his gang. We had heard Mason's name twice now and that had not got anything from Tom. What we did know was that we were closer to the girls. Our hope was that as we traveled west, we would meet up with Pa. That was all the spur we needed to get us going.

Me, I rode Tom's mare while Jamie handled the lines on the wagon. Tom perched himself on the seat with Jamie, knowing that he must wait until he was well enough to sit his own mare. That would also allow me some time with the stallion to get to know him and him me.

Our intentions were to arrive in Springfield sometime around Thanksgiving or earlier. We were undecided whether to stay there for the winter or to continue west. If we could find the girls and the gang, then we could sit for a while and then continue west to find Pa. That was the plan, but all plans are not written in stone and must change with the obstacles we might meet.

The miles rolled behind us and Tom's wound was healing nicely. His coloring was some better, but he seemed to me to be in a strange mood. Ma would have called it melancholy. Me, I just couldn't figger it. He would go hours without speaking, and then he would only grumble to hisself. With Tom like he was and Jamie not much on conversation, the three days it took to get to Poplar Bluff crept by slowly.

It had been a dry fall, and the road we traveled rolled dust over everything and us.

We hadn't traveled anytime at all before we were caked with road dust, which didn't improve Tom's or our natures. Not any at all. Tom surely did hate to get dirty. But there was one thing I noted he had not neglected ever. He always kept his guns cleaned and kept his rifle near him as he cleaned and loaded them.

"Pull 'em up, boys. We've some talking to do!" We stopped where a small creek ran beside the trail.

It was only a couple of miles to Poplar Bluff, but it was now that Tom finally decided to speak up. We were all ears as he started to speak. Maybe we would find out more of his mysterious life.

Since the small creek still had water running about knee-deep, we allowed the horses and mules to take a drink and then we turned them out for some grazing. Only after all this was done did we allow ourselves some time to knock some dust from our clothes and use a wet rag towel to clean our face and necks. Feeling some better, we hunkered down under the shade of a spreading oak near the water.

"Boys, I haven't said much till now, but we got to be prepared for what may lie before us. That's why I need to speak my mind and get it all out!"

"Prepared for what?" was our reply.

"Well, to begin with, let's start with exactly who I am. You boys have never asked, and I have never volunteered any information, but here it is. I'm your ma's youngest stepbrother. Counting on blood and all, we are no kin. But your ma's folks took me in when my own folks up and left me to die. My own ma had died of the fever, and I had it too. My pa and them no-account half brothers up and left me with your ma's parents. That's why I took my mother's last name. You would have thought my own folks would have cared more, but not them. You might say that my pa had a way of using up women. The mother of the Clayton men was the first wife to die shortly after the youngest of them was born. The Riles were the sons of wife number two from before she married up with Pa. My ma was the third or fourth wife, but the old man never kept count. Anyhow, your ma's folks were kind enough to nurse me back to health. I was only six years old then and stayed with them until I was about sixteen. For those ten years, they were all the family I knew or cared about. Your ma and pa had been married for about four or five years and had the two older girls and then you, Matt, arrived. For the next four years, your pa and grandpa spent those years trying to teach me as much as they could. Matt, you were only three or four, and Jamie, you had just been born when I up and took off. I figured that I was one mouth too many to feed. That day when I arrived at the cabin was the first time I had seen your ma since that day fourteen years ago. I knew that trouble was heading your way, I just didn't know that they were ahead me!"

"How could you have known that?" was my question.

"Well, because your pa and I had been partners on and off for quite some time."

"So where at did you see Pa last?"

"That's a fair question, Jamie. After knocking around for a few years, we met up in Richmond in early days of the war in 1861. Your dad had just left a cargo ship after serving as first mate on a voyage to South America. Now, that itself is a story to be told another time. But on the return voyage, your pa had heard a passenger talking of a gold strike somewhere in the Colorado Rockies. So when your pa and I met up in Charlestown, we decided to partner up. Our plan was to head out for the headwaters of the South Platte and Arkansas rivers around a new town called Leadville.

"Once we got geared up, we headed west. Your pa had sent a message to your Ma where and what we were going to do. We both felt sure that we would find ourselves a fortune."

"But you got to clear up something for me," Jamie posed. "What happened from the start of the war and then 1865?"

"Well you can never plan for unseen dangers and just bad luck. Your pa and I had no plan of getting caught up in the war. But that is what hit us head-on. Another time, your pa or myself will tell the rest of the story. Just understand that our plans got changed, and that is what brings us to today. I know you saw your dad in '65 as we headed west again. That was when your mom got pregnant with little Jenny. I know he only spent a day and two nights before he got back on the train heading west. Using the train was to throw off Mason and his gang off the trail. My job was to give someone else to trail and lead them anywhere except west to Colorado territory!"

It was clear to Jamie and me that Tom was leaving out some details that we ached to ask about. Yet we let him continue uninterrupted.

"On our first time out west, we made some friends who helped us in heading the right direction. We done right well until some Southern sympathizers showed up around the area of our mine. These rebels were needing money and just expected any and all Southerners to ante up. But your pa and I had other ideas. We had been breaking our backs, worked blisters on our hands and sweated blood to get what we had. We just weren't about to give it to the likes of Zack Mason and his bunch of cutthroats. It's that bunch who we're trailing, just so you know. He figured we would be beholden to him since Tobe and Frank, being family. Also, they were a part of his so-called militia. But we knew them for what they really were. They were no good thieves and murderers. They were men who would kill for the price of a drink.

"Now let me tell you about Mason. Mason was a neighbor back in Virginia and had a big hankering for your mother before she married your pa. Your pa and Mason were down and out enemies from word go because of your ma!"

Jamie and I looked at each with a question to ask, but we stopped ourselves to let Tom finish his tale. This was the most Tom had said about his or our family's past. We just let him continue with his story.

"Well, we had gotten into the habit of hiding our cache of gold nuggets and dust every two or three days. We only kept enough around to buy food and what we needed. Our plan was to load up and leave for home. Once we got far enough headed east, we would reverse back to the mine and recover our stash and be gone. All this was based on giving Mason and his bunch the slip. They needed something to do that would take them far from Colorado. But we tried our best in decoying Mason and his gang. They were sure we had taken out enough gold that it was worth their effort to stay watching for us as we tried to leave. Mason knew that we would need several mules, horses, or a wagon to haul the gold out. When we located that many animals, it would then alert Mason as to what was happening. Hiding the gold would be a better deal, at least until Mason's gang weren't waiting to steal it all from us." Tom took a breath of air and finished the story.

"The upshot was that we let it be known that I was leaving for Denver to bank our gold. Only thing, I didn't have but a single bag of dust and a mule loaded up with plain rocks. Naturally, Mason and his gang finally stopped me just before I got to Denver City. They was some peeved by not getting the whole shebang. They knew we had to have more gold than that. They'd likely would have shot me right then but your pa was right there behind them with a double-barreled shotgun. Your pa was right good at trailing man or beast, so he had trailed along behind them.

"You see, your pa hid the last bags of gold nuggets and dust in the hiding place, then he followed behind Mason and his gang, since we were all headed for Denver City. He knew that there would be trouble with Mason and his gang. Your pa was a real cautious man. He never left anything up to chance. With your pa's help, we straightened out their notion about trying to take even the one bag of gold. Once Mason and his gang took off, your dad and I headed on to Denver City. Realize this, we were intending to return to Tennessee for your ma, you boys, and the girls, even if the war was going on.

"But that was when the war caused a major problem. We had made it to Missouri and it all blew apart. We were arrested and then conscripted into a Yankee regiment and ended up fighting until just before the end of the war. With the Yankees, the choice was to join up or go straight to prison. So we joined and headed east right into the fighting. We had just sent off a packet of things to your ma before the army got in the way. It was the end of 1864 when several of us were captured at Fredericksburg. Your pa was hurt during the fighting by shrapnel that had struck a glancing blow to his head. I just decided to let myself get captured along with him so that I could take care of him. It was a dicey thing. We had already heard that as doctors go, the rebel doctors were worse than cow or dog vets. I'm sure that if I had not been with your pa, he probably would have died.

"We lay in that prison for days and weeks while your pa was out of his head. As fate would have it, Tobe had been caught with several others and ended up in the same prison. He overheard your pa carrying on about buried gold and an Indian rattle. But it was a full two weeks before your pa got well enough to stop his talking out of his head. Tobe knew exactly what your pa was talking about, for sure.

"By that time, your pa was better and there was a group of us ready to break out of that prison. We knew that news was good for us. The South was on its last leg. But we weren't about to wait until Grant and Sherman drove the final nail in the coffin of the South. Naturally, we tried to keep Tobe out of our small group of about twelve fellows we had made friends while there in the prison. No one trusted Tobe. Other prisoners had started the tunnel, and we were able to finish it and use it to escape. It was two days after our escape that we realized that Tobe had found the tunnel and had managed to slip out with our group. We should have cut his throat right then and there, but we couldn't take the time, so we just vamoosed. We knew he would eventually find Mason and his gang. I'm sure that he told Mason all the things he had heard there in the prison. Knowing that, we just had to move faster and smarter than them.

"Your pa had left that Injun rattle with you boys in among those presents he sent the day we were conscripted into the army. It had a map on the inside that would lead us to where we had buried the gold. But Mason and his gang were our biggest problem. As soon as they could get together, they would be hot on the trail for the gold and us!

"That's why your pa headed straight for Colorado and the gold while I was to fetch the rest of the family."

"What happened to Pa?"

"Mason and his gang tried to follow your pa all over the South. He took them everywhere except near your home. Your pa thought that he had finally lost Mason, so that was why he traveled straight to the cabin. That's when you both saw him last. He left and headed west and has been there ever since. I was to wait some time and then gather the family together and head west. There were problems that occurred that took me more than a year and half to do my part! Gilbert was part of that problem. There are several stories that would take too much time to relate. Just know that I kept trying to get to you all. I got delayed more than once. There was nothing I could change!

"What may have happened to your pa, I have no clue. Whether he made it out west or not, I just don't know. Mason had spies everywhere. That was just one of our problems. Way I figure it, he may have got hurt or killed. Otherwise, he'd a been back by now. Maybe in Springfield we can hear some news about him."

With that, Tom stooped down and finished washing up. Standing, he slapped off the road dust and his melancholy mood at the same time.

"You boys didn't ask about the last name. It is Wilson. I borrowed your mother's last name. Sounded better than Clayton!" With that, he finished with his cleanup.

Chapter 11

Tom's speech had lodged in our minds for the time being, but his words also created more questions that needed answers at another time and place. Hopefully, sooner rather than later.

Jamie and I looked at each other for a long time before we silently joined him at the creek. We washed ourselves off the dirt and dust of the road, and with a swipe of the hand, we brushed as much as we could from our pants and shirts.

Jamie gave me a nudge with his elbow and said quietly, "Poplar Bluff must be some place. Tom's taking extra care at cleaning up."

Jamie's words drew my eyes to where Tom was sitting propped against a wagon wheel. He had his guns laid out around him as he cleaned and oiled each weapon and carefully reloaded each one after wiping each cartridge. It seemed like a wise thing, so we followed his example. We had to be ready for whatever might be waiting for us. Little did we know that this town would leave its mark on all of us forever. Looking back on what had happened, I had a notion that my life was never to be quiet or pleasant again, but it was to be filled with violence, smoke, and lead. Hopefully, someday, there would be a time of love with someone, somewhere, too.

Tom got our attention and made just one more observation.

"Never hurts to be prepared, whenever. Towns have had a way of being full of surprises!" To that, we could agree, particularly because of our previous experiences.

We mounted up and headed into Poplar Bluff. It was a town still in the process of rebuilding following the war. There had been a considerable amount of guerilla fighting in the area during the end of the recent strife, and because of that, the town had its own problems.

Many folks had left during the fighting and were just now returning. Many still had homes, farms, and businesses and were trying to get back into making a living.

The town itself was located on the bluffs west of the Black River. It was a place not too distant from one of Solomon Kittrell's tanning yards and a whiskey still. According to Tom, Mr. Kittrell had been the area's first known permanent white resident sometime in 1819. His ability to get along with the Injuns of the area had encouraged others so that by 1850, there was a thriving community here in the territory everyone was calling Missouri.

Tom seemed to be honed to a point, and what he was feeling, Jamie and I felt the same. So with that in mind, we sat up a bit straighter entering the town. Tom spoke softly to the two us.

"Let's keep our eyes and ears peeled for any untoward activities!"

If anything was to happen, we knew to keep our eyes on the folks lining the street. These folks were rarely quiet, which left us unsettled. Something was waiting for us. I could feel it in the air.

This quietness hung over us as we tied up at the hitch rail. We were just across the street from the general store. There was a part of me that liked the town and its people. Another part of me was wound up tight and waiting for whatever was going to happen.

The sounds and smells of the town were rather pleasant. Hearing the steady beat of the blacksmith's hammer filled the air as he hammered at some piece of work on his anvil. A new building was going up down the street and the smell of the fresh sawed wood left a pungent odor to mix with all the other smells filling the morning. The sawdust seemed to hang in the still air as we stood watching the men working on the building.

"Jamie, stay here with the horses and the wagon. Keep your eyes peeled for any trouble. Matt, you come with me. We will have us a chat with the local sheriff. Maybe he can tell us if the girls or Mason and his gang has been around."

"All right, Tom. Jest don't be too long" was all Jamie had to say.

Tom and I made our way down the boardwalk to the sheriff's office. Folks along the way seemed to be giving us the stare, like they had been expecting something to happen, either with us or caused by us. Me, I just kept trying to keep any nervousness away and hung on to my anger to keep my mind clear.

"Tom, what you reckon is the problem with the folks in this town? They seem to know about us and are expecting something to happen. These women sure are giving me the evil eye!"

"It must be you, Matt. They just haven't seen a fine young man armed with so many weapons before. Maybe, they figure you are here to start another war. Just you stay calm and friendly. We'll see what the sheriff can tell us."

With that said, we arrived at the sheriff's office.

"How do, Sheriff!" Tom said as we entered the office.

The door had been propped open to let some air in the office. The sheriff didn't raise his eyes up from reading a poster as we entered.

"Tolerable." Then he looked up and seemed some startled. "What can I do for you gents?"

"We're interested in some information, sheriff."

"Well, trot out your question and we'll see what we can say to it!"

It was then that we could see that he had been reading a recent Wanted flyer. With his full attention on us, I could see his piercing blue eyes and his dusky color. Everything about this old-timer spoke of a man who could only speak the truth, even when faced with death. There was no fear in him, and he was one who would never give up on the trail on those who broke the law.

Tom then proceeded to tell our story and got to asking about Zach Mason and his gang and our two sisters. While they talked, I had leaned against the door jamb so that I could keep an eye on Jamie, the horses, the wagon, and the street. I had just turned to look back toward the street and I could see that trouble was coming right to Jamie.

"Tom, you finish talking to the sheriff. Me, I'm heading back to the wagon and give Jamie a hand."

Tom threw me a questioning look. "You sure you don't need my help?"

"Nope. This is one time that I can handle things." Deep inside, I did not feel near as confident as I sounded.

I could hear the sheriff's remark to Tom as I walked down the walk.

"Listen, feller, don't you think you should lend a hand with those youngsters?"

"The only person who needs any help are those who will need the doc or burying after the fight is done! One more thing. That is no boy walking down the street. He's full grown. He's the one to be feared!"

Walking down the walk, I felt a certain calmness come over me. I changed hands with the rifle to free my gun hand. Without thinking I raised and lowered the handgun to free it from sticking in the holster after slipping the thong off the hammer. It all seemed so natural.

I could see that Jamie was in a tough spot. There were two shaggy saddle bums trying to hooraw Jamie. By that I meant they were trying to bait Jamie into getting angry, so they could start a shooting.

I could hear them talking to Jamie, wanting to know where Tom or myself were. Jamie decided it was time to speak up as I got closer.

"You fellas was asking for Tom or my brother. My brother is here now. Right behind you in fact."

It took a second or two for the fact that I was behind them settled in their thick heads. Their hands were already on the handles of their pistols. They knew they had to turn and look at me and then put their backs to Jamie. They were both fools and had no clue what to do. So they decided to make a choice, which ended up a bad one, even worse.

I had stopped at about ten feet from them when they decided to pivot toward me. Each had started to draw their guns. I had given them more time than I should have, but I gave them their try.

Guns started roaring at the blink of an eye. I didn't even remember drawing my holstered gun as I stood facing the outlaws. They were both in the dirt, but I just kept my eyes on them still the same.

That was the day that I put to use what Tom had taught me. I kept my eyes on the targets, letting nothing distract me. It was good for me and not for those two.

After only a few seconds, the street was quiet again. I was pushing the spent shells out and had reloaded within seconds. Four shells lay on the street. Two shots for each man. I had tried to shoot to disarm them rather than kill them. Their guns were ruined, and there was a shot to the arm of each man. I thought at least one had gotten off a shot at me, I thought, but it had missed to the left of my head.

I quickly looked to see that Jamie was all right then turned to look behind to my left. It was then I could see a man lying in the dust of the alley. A rifle was there in the dirt near to his hand.

"Think he is dead, Matt?"

I crossed the street to the alley, bending down before answering. "Yes, Jamie. He is very dead. That was some good shooting."

"He was going to back shoot you, Matt!"

By then, Tom and the sheriff arrived and took in the scene. Me, I was just trying to keep calm and keep my hands steady as possible. The nerves inside were still shaking, but no one could see that. I was still scanning over the crowd that had gathered around as Tom had taught us.

"Did any of you folks see what happened?" the sheriff asked the crowd.

One old man spoke and said, "Best shooting I's ever seen, sheriff. These two youngsters were only defending theyselves. These no-account saddle bums were primed to kill them both. Fact is, these two already had their guns out when they were turning to face this young man."

The sheriff gave us a wink before he went down on one knee to question one of the wounded men.

"Who sent you here to do this? Speak up, man. Would you die with this on your conscience?"

The sheriff put his ear where none of us could hear what the injured man had to say. After just a few minutes, the doc arrived and started patching their wounds. He finally declared for all to hear that they would live long enough to be hung. It was a joke for the folks since both wounded men had thought they were going to die.

The sheriff had risen and met Tom's eyes. He briefly looked around the crowd to find those he needed.

"Sam, you, and Jeffers, help Doc get these two to his office and then to the jail. You know where the keys are and lock them both up. Doc's ready now. Stanford, you can take care of the dead one."

Then he turned to Tom. "Well, sir, you were right. These three were part of Mason's gang. He's surely determined to eliminate you gents from his trail and his life permanent. Was I you three, I'd be extree careful. As I was telling you before the interruption, the rest of the group passed through here three days ago. They were headed in the direction of Springfield. If you was to hustle right along, you should be able to catch up with them before they get to Springfield!"

He fixed Tom with a quizzical eye. "Iffen that's your goal! Remember, there be several trails that they could be taking. Don't let them give you the slip. They would sure love it iffen you boys got past them, if you know what I mean?"

Tom stood for a minute, considering things before he replied.

"Well, sheriff, do you need either of these young men for this fracas?"

"Not likely! It seems to be an open and shut case to me. You boys should try hard to fight shy of anymore killing, at least for today. But iffen you meet up with any of Zack Mason or his gang, feel free to shoot as straight as you can. This country needs less of his kind."

Jamie and I looked at each other, and Jamie held up his two hands with eight fingers up and then dropped three. "That leaves five! They should feel the heat from us following them."

"Yes, Jamie. I can feel them out there. They are waiting for us! I just hope the girls don't give up on us. They must know we are coming."

Chapter 12

It was only a few minutes and Jamie and I had the wagon loaded in front of the store while Tom walked over to converse with the sheriff once again. He planned to meet us in a short time. Jamie and I took a minute to walk into the store. It appeared that the shooting was the main talk of everyone in the store. They seemed to give us a quick glance and looked away. I wasn't sure whether it was fear or awe after we just had a gunfight and survived.

"Jamie, I believe that I have a dime on me. How's about some candy?"

"Sounds good to me. I've had a sweet tooth for something to suck on! Maybe some horehound would be tasty or even some peppermint."

With that thought in mind, we wandered over to the counter where the candy and stuff could be found. Jamie just naturally got in too big of a hurry and bumped into a mighty, pretty young lady. Her arms where full of packages, which went flying with his bump.

"I swear!" she said as she bent over to pick up the lost packages. She kept trying to get a stray curl back under her bonnet while picking up her packages.

Being the gentleman like I was, I quickly stooped to help her gather the packages back up. With the last one, we both tried to pick it up at the same time. Our hands met, and our eyes met for the first time. It was the longest second ever in my life. Those were the prettiest blue eyes I had ever seen. I just lost myself for a few seconds and continued to hold on to her hand.

"Excuse me, miss. You'll have to pardon my little brother. He doesn't pay much attention to anything or people in his way, particularly when it comes to candy."

Then I remembered having her hand in mine. She was just so gorgeous. She had the bluest eyes that I had ever seen and a body to match. She had a face that ranked up with the angels (that is, if the angels had a few freckles around a button nose) and lips that seemed to always want to smile and hair that reminded me of the color of flame as it lay curled about her face. It was a face that I would never, ever forget. Within just a few seconds, my heart burst open and placed her face where there had been nothing but rage and revenge. Maybe, perhaps love could be found there?

"Well, sir, it is quite all right. Thank you very much for your help. However, you can let go of my hand now!"

Instantly, I dropped her hand. I had not realized that I was still holding her hand in my own. In just a second, I stood and yanked off my hat.

"Miss, you'll have to forgive me as well for my lapse of manners. It has been some time since we've been around any womenfolk. But that's no excuse for poor manners. Let's try and start over again. My name is Matthew Allison. Most folks just call me Matt."

"Pleased to make your acquaintance, Mr. Allison. My name is Audrey Parks. My daddy calls me Red because of this awful red hair. Everyone must think it fits since they all call me that. What do you think, Mr. Allison, I'm sorry, Matt?"

"Well, if I had a choice, I'd just call you Audrey! Seems a right pretty name. But don't get me wrong. I also think your hair to be very beautiful, if you'll forgive my forwardness. I believe that red hair fits you fine."

I hope I did not sound as stupid as I sounded to myself. I couldn't believe my ears. Here I was starting to sound like some Don Juan or something. A real lady's man. Ouch. I was the guy who generally ended up all tongue-tied and left-footed around any females, even my own sisters.

About that time, Jamie figured it was time to save me, so he trailed over and asked for the dime that had been burning a hole in my pocket that originally brought us into the store in the first place.

It was then that Audrey's father came into the store. He was a giant of a man. He must have been all of six and a half feet tall. A person could tell because he had to duck under the door to enter. If he weighed an ounce less than three hundred pounds, or I'd eat my hat. He was one big man for sure. But as I was to learn later, he was bigger in ways that don't always show but do count when it involved people or difficult situations.

"Who is this young man, Red?"

"Father, this is Matt Allison. Matt, this is my father, Elijah Parks!"

"Pleased to meet you, sir" was all I got out before my hand was being crushed by his massive grip. I tried my best to return the grip, but my hands were too small in comparison to his to gain a purchase on his huge hand. As I glanced at his face, I could see a twinkle in his eyes.

He continued to smile at me.

"You'll do, boy. Oh yes, you'll do! Wait just a minute now. Is your father's name John?"

Before I could answer, I saw Tom coming through the door like a man with a purpose. He stopped at the door and searched the store for us with his eyes. Once we made eye contact, he realized that there was no cause for concern. He relaxed just a mite. That was one of the things about Tom that I had come to realize about him. He was constantly on the alert for trouble. Tom was constantly preparing himself for action. His hands were always hanging loose, usually resting on the butt of his handgun, while his eyes were always moving around the room or area we might be in. Ready for anything and everything.

As Tom stepped in the door, he saw who we were talking to. I saw his face brighten up like seeing the sun on a cloudy day. It was then I saw a wicked glint come into his eyes. He walked up slowly behind Mr. Parks and his daughter without them knowing he was there. Tom then extended his index finger into the middle of Mr. Parks's back and pressed hard.

"Up with your hands!"

Mr. Parks's hands flew up without a thought. In just a second, his worried frown quickly changed to a wide grin as recognition came over him. He whirled around with a speed that belied his great size and he had Tom in a bear hug that would have cracked a lesser person's spine. Just as quickly, he dropped Tom to the floor and slapped him on the back with a grin.

"I shoulda known it was you, Tom. You're the only person I know who is fool enuff to try and scare me like that."

"Eli, old friend. What are you doing here, of all places? Last I saw you was when we all escaped from that dang prison. You seemed to be right anxious to get away then!"

"Of course, I was making tracks for home. The wife and children needed their father. I don't think anyone wanted to stay in that prison, certainly not me!"

"How is your wife doing? Hope she is doing all right now?"

"Yes, she is doing as well as can be. Howsomever, she needs a little warmer climate. Someone told us of the hot springs down in Northwest Arkansas. They say that they help to ease a person's aches and pains, so we plan to make a stop there before we get to our last stop."

"So that explains why you are here, but where is your final stop?"

"Well we un's are heading to Indian Territory. I've got a foreman's job on Mr. Brand's ranch in the Nations. He's an old friend of my wife, Lettie's, family."

"Eli, that sounds great. It sure fits right with plans I'd like to discuss with you private like. This might work out for all of us. How's about we step over to the saloon yonder and quench our thirst and discuss some plans!"

"You first, Tom."

Turning to Audrey, Mr. Parks gave her a list of things to finish in the store.

"Get those packages into the wagon whilst I palaver with Tom. And Red, don't you be leading these young men astray, hear! And find what else your ma needs anything else done before we leave."

With that, they walked quickly across the street to the saloon, talking as they went. We could hear their loud laughter as we strolled down the dirt street, leaving the store behind us. Audrey just naturally walked along at my side. Her that close made me feel like I was walking on air.

"It looks like Tom and your dad are old friends. Ain't that something?" was all I could think to say.

There was just a touch of breeze, and the warmth of the early fall day seemed perfect. A calmness lay on the street that so recently had been filled with violence and death. An old dog was scratching fleas while a couple of hens were pecking at the gravel near the road. Any thoughts of the recent shooting were lost from my mind as I enjoyed one of the most perfect afternoons of my eighteen years. Maybe it was perfect because my present idea of perfection was shaped by the lovely young lady who walked by my side.

We got to their wagon and handed the packages to her mother, sitting on the tailgate with the little ones sitting around her. Audrey introduced us around to them all.

"Matt, would you like to walk to the stables with me? My horse lost a shoe and it should be done!"

"Sure, I'd be delighted to go with you!" was all I could stammer.

Being with Audrey made my tongue turn into a slab of bark. I was getting all nervy around her. I sure surprised myself that I could talk at all. We ended up walking side by side toward the stable with Jamie trailing behind us about fifteen feet. Not so close he could hear us clear, but close enough to help if there were any other difficulties.

"Your pony is ready, young lass. Would you want her saddled now?"

This was my chance to do something for Audrey.

"I'll do it. Just allow me."

"Why, thank you, Matt!"

With that said, I saddled the pony and led her to the door.

"If you'd like, I'll walk along with you back to the wagon, unless it's a problem?"

"That would please me greatly, Matt!"

So we headed back to the wagon with the pony walking behind us when Tom and Mr. Parks emerged from the saloon. We arrived about the same time. Jamie had walked slowly down to our wagon and stood there waiting for the news to come to him while he guarded the area. Tom and Mr. Parks seemed real pleased with themselves for they were laughing and slapping each other on the back.

"Well, you young folks best get this rig ready to head out because we're leaving in less than ten minutes," stated Mr. Parks.

"Oh, Pa, are we going to travel with these fellas?" One of the little ones yelled.

"You betcha, kiddos. Further than you can imagine!"

Tom quickly returned to the store and picked up the few supplies we needed. Jamie and I helped him carry them to the wagon and packed them away. With that, we pulled the canvas down tight to cover everything, and off we went.

"Well, boys, fortune has smiled on us. Let's be on our way. Ole Eli won't be waiting around. Let's get with it!"

With that, Tom climbed up beside Jamie on the driver's seat and took the reins. I was already sitting the saddle of my own horse. This horse and I had come to an understanding. The stallion would behave himself, and I would treat him occasionally with parts of an apple. Duke seemed a good name for the stallion, so Duke and I were riding alongside Mr. Parks's wagon.

Tom had tied his two mares with lead lines to the back of our wagon. For me it felt good to leave that town. Death had come and gone so suddenly. It still rattled me some, but not enough to cause any big deal in my mind.

"It sure will be nice to have some company, right, guys?" Jamie yelled over the sound of the wagons.

Tom glanced over toward him and replied with a twinkle in his eyes.

"Yes, Jamie. Only ole Matt ain't concerned about you or me having any company. He's got his mind on something else." Tom laughed out loud for the first time since back at the cabin.

I could hear every word that was said, but I just grinned and said nothing. On the inside, however, I was shouting a resounding yes. A thousand times, yes. It was the first time that I felt this good and not so worked up over the situation we were in.

As it turned out, our time with Mr. Parks and his family was going to be longer than we had at first expected. We were still hopeful of finding some more recent evidence of our sisters and those who had them. There was still blood ahead us, without a doubt. We could count on it. The plan was to make sure it was not ours but the renegades who still had our sisters.

Chapter 13

The trip to Springfield went without a hitch. There were no further attempts on our lives as we passed through the many small villages along the way. It was as close to a peaceful, happy time as the three of us and the Parks family had experienced in nine months now.

The stop in Springfield was just long enough for Mrs. Parks and the younger children to stop and visit some family.

The three of us had come to admire Mrs. Parks. She was a robust lady with sparkling blue eyes to match those of Audrey. It only took a glance to see that her health hadn't been as good as it should. But she was getting some better, no doubt. Even so, she depended on Audrey to chase those two young towheaded boys, who were six and ten years old.

Leaving Springfield, we headed southwest toward the Nations. With the women and children along, it made for shorter days.

Along the way, Tom kept us on our toes from morning until after dark. If he wasn't telling us about horses and cattle and such, he was covering fighting and tactics. He was always trying to present different problems and how best to deal with them.

Jamie and I tried to listen to every word. We knew that we were like babes in the woods and we needed any and all the help we could get.

It was hard to describe the time that Audrey and I were able to spend time together. Sometimes on the trail we would ride together on the wagon with her doing her share of the driving. Sometimes I would use the reins to give her a break. Other times we would ride horseback along the trail. Sometimes in the front and then sometimes in the back.

It seemed natural for us to share many personal things between us. I never thought that I would share these things with anyone else, certainly not a young lady like Audrey. It kind of grew on me, being with Audrey. I wasn't sure it was love or not, but it sure did feel good to be with her. I could remember how being loved by Mom and loving her back, but these feelings were different. Time would tell what would grow.

We had been on the trail for three weeks when Jamie and I had the first chance to talk in private. We had just finished a wrestling match and had paused to take a break for a drink. As we sat on the ground, Jamie just had to speak up first.

"When is Tom going to ease up on us, Matt?"

"Your guess is as good as mine, Jamie. He's got a burr under his blanket, and it just keeps digging in. It's like he can't tell us enough or teach us enough for some reason. Maybe he figures we got to grow up sooner than later."

Jamie's reply was quick and to the point.

"Me, I think he's planning to leave us and go hunting for Pa. He still believes that Pa is still alive. Because of that, he's been some worried that we might miss connecting with Pa, particularly since we're headed toward Indian Territory."

"But Jamie, we left word in Springfield for Pa to head southwest and meet us. Tom also spoke with several who are headed toward St. Louis. They will spread the word to others. Somehow he will get the word."

"But that's the point. Tom has calculated the time Pa needed to get back to their claim and the time he would need to return. Tom knows he is late and by a lot."

"Let's sit down with Tom after supper and discuss whatever plans he has in mind. We haven't forgotten about Ardith and Helen! I feel that we are close and they must know by now that we are looking for them. We just aren't going to let them down!"

A quick word with Tom was all that was needed to set up the evening discussion. However, the afternoon seemed to drag on and on. We were all feeling the atmosphere at supper, and we couldn't eat fast enough. It was time to talk.

Tom knew we were anxious, and I could see he was the same. The Parks family also felt they were to be a big part of what the future would hold. This was a drama that included us all.

"Let's all gather around the fire and get things out in the open for all to hear and understand where we are at. I know you boys are all anxious, so let's get to it!"

As we found a place to sit, Jamie and I both tried to interrupt, but Tom wasn't allowing it.

"Now hear me out, and then you will get your turn. We need to get some word from your pa. He should have already been back. I expected to meet him in Springfield. But it is obvious that he was not there, and no news was left with those he would have trusted with that kind of information. Having all that gold can be a real temptation for all kinds of people, particularly Zach Mason and his gang. Howsomever, we got no way of knowing what has happened along the way with your pa, and there is still the matter of your sisters and the Mason gang. We got to get the girls away from those lowlifes before anymore hurt can come to the girls. The Lord hisself only knows what sort of torment and pain they have endured."

Tom's pause was punctuated by the snapping of a knot in the fire as we were huddled around. The fire sent a mass of embers floating through the clear night air. I could feel the crisp, cold air that seemed to constantly gnaw at whatever side was turned from the fire.

"But," he continued, "I done changed my mind several times. We are all going to Brand's ranch with Eli and his family. But we'll only spend a few days to rest up. Then we hit the trail to find Mason, if we haven't found them before then. We will leave the wagon with them and take only what we can carry on our horses. We only want the essentials. Nothing that will hold us back.

"The girls have to be the first thing, and then on to find your pa. I had thought that I would go on alone, but you boys have shown me that I can depend on you both in any difficulty. So if we have to separate then we will!"

With that said, Tom turned to Eli and spoke directly with him. "Eli, do you or your missus have anything to ask or add?"

"No, Tom. You've got a real tough job to do and little time to do it in. Either way you want to do things, you and the boys will always be welcome to stay with us for as long as you need. The missus and I figure these are right good young men. We certainly can understand their desire to find their sisters and pa."

"Well, if that's settled then we best get to sleep. We'll be in Indian Territory in a week or two. The ranch lies only four or five days after that. Getting to the ranch is going to feel downright pleasant after the change in the weather. We only have four weeks till Thanksgiving. So it will be great to have a house with a roof over our heads and a fireplace and such to be thankful about. With that said, let's say good night. Come along, Mother. Let's get these young'uns to bed."

As we each said our goodnights, my eyes were drawn to Audrey. She had sat silently through the whole discussion. Her hands were demurely folded in her lap. Maybe now she would speak her mind to me.

She came around the fire and sat by me on the four-foot log, putting her hands in mine. It was several moments before she spoke. It was only with great effort that I could gaze into her eyes.

"Audrey, you're making me some nervous! Tell me what is on your mind!"

Up to this point we had shied away from any kind of intimacy other than holding hands. To my mind it had just seemed the proper thing to keep things simple. Maybe it was that I wasn't sure that I could trust myself around her. I had a difficult time knowing what to say or do that would express my true feelings. This was a new experience for me, and I think it was for Audrey also.

"No, Matt. I'm just concerned, is all. I'm just trying to memorize your face in my mind, the way your hair has a certain texture to it that reflects the light of the sun. I want to remember that and more. I want to remember the sound of your voice. It has a special quality to it. Not harsh nor light but commanding. Everyone listens when you are talking. I want to remember the way you walk and how you look on your horse. Every day, up till now, I have watched and tried to memorize each detail. When you leave, I'll remember all those little things that make you, you."

"Why would you feel that way about me?" I managed to say even though it felt that someone was sucking all the air out of my lungs. It was then that I noticed everyone had left us alone.

"Because I know when you leave, it will leave a hole in my heart. It will be quite a long time before I see you again. I don't want to forget one thing about you. Our time together hasn't been all that long, yet I have treasured every minute."

"Audrey, I—" was all I got out when she kissed me.

I was so amazed, but I also felt like a weight had been lifted from my shoulders and some strange but wonderful feelings were running through my body.

"Matt, Mama knows how I feel. She says a little boldness never hurt. I may only be sixteen, but I know what my heart feels, and I think you feel the same!"

"Yes, Audrey. Thinking about leaving you and the family is making my heart ache near as much as when Mama died. But I can't ask you to wait for me, knowing what I must face along with Jamie and Tom. You're marrying age and all, and who knows how long I'll be gone."

Without stopping to think about her response, Audrey answered with another kiss that I will remember for the rest of my life.

Pulling away from me, she answered, "Matt, you don't have to ask anything. I have already pledged my heart to you. I will wait as long as it will take. There is no one who can replace you in my heart. Do what you must do, but do it as quickly as you can. Stay safe and return to me when you are ready. I will be waiting!"

With another quick kiss, she walked back to the family wagon and her bed. What I should have said was what ran through my brain. *I love you!*

My last words to her as she rose to walk away was "I'll be back, Audrey. You can count on it! I'll be back. Don't you forget me neither!"

I kept repeating it in my mind over and over. I'll be back. I'll be back.

I couldn't hear what was said, but I could hear Audrey and her mother were having a quiet talk. Whatever it was about, I knew that some of it was about the two of us. So as I lay on my blanket and saddle, I tried to sleep but sleep was hard to find until it found me late into the night. Tomorrow will be another day. It was time to begin hunting. Hunting for Ardith and Helen. Then to find Pa.

Chapter 14

It was hard when none of us had a clue what Zach Mason and his gang were up to. Without a crystal ball, we felt that we were within a day's ride. It was time to get down to finding them. If we had the girls safe, then we could go after Pa, gold or no gold. We must keep in mind, all the time, that Mason and his gang would take some killing.

Arkansas was quite a place to visit, especially following the recent civil conflict. We had some neighbors from back home who moved out to Arkansas during and after the war. The Duncans or the Clarks would be the places to go if we needed any help. They were friends from back in Tennessee and always had a place at the table for those who had need. Somebody had said that they were down in Yell County. Might be a place to stop before we headed west to Brand's ranch.

Hot Springs was a comforting place. It was a coming town. We had heard that around this town, there were neighbors as close as a half mile. Many folks felt it was getting right crowded in this country. We thought it was nice country, but we were on a mission, not to settle down yet.

I felt like being an outsider, and I knew it was time to get going. Audrey and I had been able to spend some time together, but I was just not much fun. There were too many things on my mind. And as Tom reminded us every day, keep at least one eye on the crowds, we might meet someone we want to see first and avoid any more trouble than needed.

"Audrey, do you reckon that it's wrong for me to have fun? You know what I mean. We must find the sisters and then Pa. I still have Mama's promise hanging over me. We got to find them all!"

"I'm not sure I understand or know how you feel, Matt. I think that your mother would be very upset if you were not enjoying your life just because she was gone. From all that you have told me, she seemed to be the kind of person who enjoyed life to the fullest. She would want you to do the same. Your life could be over just as quickly, so you need to embrace all that life gives you and take all the joy you can in the time that God has given you."

"Maybe, but I know that before I cash out, those who caused her death will be dead and in their graves long before I get there."

"But don't you know, Matt, that revenge will not bring her back to you or Jamie? Nor will it bring back your baby sister or give back all this time that your sisters have been apart from you. You must get over this revengeful attitude. There are times I can see the signs in your eyes. Try to build on something new. Something fresh and uplifting. Maybe, think about you and me. It surely makes me smile every time I think of you or being around you. Do you understand what I'm saying?"

In my heart, I knew exactly what she was saying. Most times I think the same way, but then I get reminded of Ma and everything that had happened. Then hate and anger would just come over me. Trying to have thoughts of a wife, children, a new home, or anything along those lines quickly were pushed out by my feelings of revenge. I just didn't have any time for new thoughts or ideas. It was time to ride.

My only response to Audrey was short. "I'll try. Just give me some time. I'll try my best!"

We had camped just outside Hot Springs while Mrs. Parks availed herself of the curative nature of the springs. We had been there nigh on to a week when Mr. Parks announced that Mrs. Parks was feeling more like her old self and was ready to travel on to the ranch in Indian Territory.

"We've discussed it up one side and down the other, and it's time we were moving on. Any objections? Hearing none, we all better adjourn to our bedrolls for the night so's we can be up at the crack of dawn. Let's be ready."

With that said, he grabbed the two youngsters by their ears and commenced to haul them to the wagon. He pointed to their beds that lay under the wagon. "There'll be no shenanigans from you two tonight. Understand?"

The two, together, answered, "Yes, Pa. Jest let go of our ears. I... I mean, we understand clearly, sir."

Mrs. Parks turned to Jamie, Audrey, and I. "You young folks try to get to bed as soon as possible. Morning will come early!"

Ever the polite one, Audrey replied, "Yes, Ma. I'll be in a bit."

We only lingered around the fire with just small talk. We finally left the fire to Tom. He was still sitting there on the ground, leaning back against a log, as Jamie and I were almost to sleep. Tom seemed to be having some deep thoughts, and he did not want anyone or anything bothering him. His hands were clasped together as he leaned on his stump.

Just like me, he had his own demons to wrestle with. My prayer was that we both win this fight and never let what had happened to us change us into demons ourselves. We must fight it every day. I hadn't thought much of the good Lord, but right now seemed a good time to ask for his help.

Chapter 15

The trail we were on headed south and then west. Within a few days, we crossed the Grand River. Once we were on its western bank, we headed south to find Mr. Brand's ranch. Brand's ranch was rather notorious as Tom had heard from folks along the trail. Mr. Brand was one of the first white settlers in this area. He had come to the territory around 1830. That was before the Indian relocation had started. The Indian tribes along the East Coast were the first to be sent to the area that was then called Indian Territory.

Mr. Brand had worked with his partner, Henry Barbour. They had established an outpost on the Verdigris River north of the Three Forks area. This was the area where the Grand River and the Verdigris flowed into the Arkansas River. Brand later married a full-blooded Cherokee woman, which then allowed him to stay in the territory. His marriage allowed him to own land. It was this relationship that kept him there long after the fur trade had petered out.

We had pushed extra hard, hoping to shorten the distance on the following day. Sundown was early, so we stopped at a clearing. Jamie and I started to gather firewood and then jumped right in and helped Audrey and her mother get things ready for supper. We had been raised to be polite and mannerly, but we also were hungry and that pushed us as well.

With a hand to the small of her back to ease some pain, she hollered out, "Coffee's on, Eli! Tom, you and these young men should sit on down and let Audrey and I get the meal prepared. Matt, you and Jamie were a great help! You, young men, are good examples for my boys to see that when something needs to be done without being told."

Earlier in the day, Tom had ridden off from the trail to do some hunting to supplement the food supplies. He had shot a nice young spiked deer. He had skinned and cut the deer into four haunches to bring back to camp. He ended giving half to a pair of Cherokee braves who he had met on the hunt. They were glad because that much food would keep the family fed for at least a week or more. Tom knew that helping them out would make them friends, and we might need them later. The young braves filled Tom about the trail ahead, and there might be trouble waiting.

Mrs. Parks was in the process of frying some of the deer meat into steaks. Audrey, on the other hand, was slicing several potatoes and onions into another pan for frying. Those were smells that were almost intoxicating after a long day's riding.

Jamie and I sat close to the fire and nursed a hot cup of coffee in our gloved hands, letting the kinks ease out of our very tired and sore muscles. Tom and Eli had chosen to stake out the horses.

As I sat there, I felt that something was out of kilter. I'd been hearing sounds that didn't belong. Slowly, I turned my back to the fire, closed my eyes, and tried to shut out the sounds of the campfire and cooking and the children playing close by. I slowly stood and walked a few feet away from the camp, straining my ears. Then Jamie stood with me and looked toward the same direction I was. We both stood there straining our ears.

"Matt, I think we're hearing someone talking or yelling."

"That is a woman's voice!" was my reply.

In just a few moments, we could then hear the words more clearly. It was a woman's voice, and she was calling out for help.

"Help me! Somebody help me, please!"

We both took off running toward the voice like wild horses. We looked at one another, and we both knew who that voice belonged to.

It was Ardith! She was the elder of our two sisters who had been missing since that fatal day back in Tennessee. Jamie and I had both thrown the cups away as we headed into the woods, hoping to find her. We both knew that she was in trouble and needed us. I gave Tom a shout as Jamie and I rushed by him.

"Tom, that shout sounds like Ardith! I would bet money on that!"

"Slow down, boys. We will find her! We must be ready to do what needs to be done. Slow right down and keep your voices down. Maybe we will surprise her when we find her. That gang is with her, remember? Hear me?"

With that said, we all grabbed up our rifles. I followed his lead with removing the thong off my handgun.

"They are over here," Jamie called. "Over here. Help's over here!"

Jamie was the first one to reach her. He ran across the clearing, standing over Ardith lying on the ground. Jamie was looking at the opening that Ardith had made through the rough weeds and lower limbs of trees. Without a word, Tom and I split up, heading around the clearing to see who was following her. Jamie helped Ardith cross to the far side of the clearing.

Ardith made it that far and was just sitting up, talking to Jamie as he kept his eyes on the trail. Tom and I could hear everything that was said, but we kept quiet and remained at our vantage points, standing behind large trees across from each other.

"Be careful, Jamie! Where is Matt? We need some help. These men are animals. No one is safe. They have been following me for an hour or more. I got lost, and then I got to here. I'm just used up. I don't think I could walk another step!"

With a look toward Tom, I stepped behind a larger tree and waited for the ones who had been following Ardith. This bunch were making enough noise for an army. I could barely hear Jamie telling Ardith to crawl behind him and get behind the tree. I leaned my rifle against the tree and made sure my pistol was loose.

It was only two or three minutes when the gang arrived at the clearing. They were a disheveled and dirty band of thieves and killers. They just stood there glaring at Jamie. All they wanted was Ardith, and some young boy was standing in the way.

"Listen up, boy. Where's that girl gone to?"

The leader was only average in height but was unnaturally broad through the shoulders and arms. His coat was a couple of sizes too small so that he was unable to fasten the buttons. This only exaggerated his immense arms and shoulders. His face quickly got my attention. His face could not be forgotten. His face was covered with a beard of ebony curls, allowing his lips, eyes, and tip of his nose to be seen. There was something about his eyes that reminded me of Tom's, but they were different also. Then it dawned on me. This man's eyes were the eyes of a stone-cold killer. This had to be Tom's only remaining half brother, Isaiah. He made the mistake of talking to Jamie when I stepped out and got his attention.

"Hey, fool! You need to talk to me. I'm the one who will deal with you personally. I've never liked nor allowed dirty vermin to stink up the air."

He turned and saw me.

"Now I remember you two boys. I wish to God that your pappy were here to see you both die. It should have happened months ago. Howsomever, this seems a good time for dying. I do declare."

Tom then chimed in for all to hear him from the other side of the clearing.

"Isaiah, you have just one chance to drop you weapons and then turn around and leave here alive. Let the other sister free if you have her, and then go back to some hole you call home. There is this one chance and only one."

"My, my, my! You really have me scared. It's my guess, I hear you, dear, sweet half brother, Tom. I can understand why you are here! Speak up, Tom! Should I turn around and face you or take care of this wet behind the ear youngster?"

"Yes, it's me. But don't worry about me. Matt has already spoken for you. You will have your hands with Matt there. There are only five of you against three of us. Matt is probably more than you can handle. He is probably good for at least one more, at least. I would really consider what you plan to do here!"

To get his attention back on me, I said, "You must have always been the ugliest of the bunch. So what's your choice? It's just you and me. So what is it going to be?"

While we were talking, Jamie had handed Ardith his handgun.

"Listen, boy. You don't scare me, not at all. I will kill both you and your pissant brother, so help me God!"

Ardith spoke softly from behind Jamie, "He's the one who took me the most. It was him who throwed me to the others and beat me when I didn't move quick enough to suit him."

With that, I knew the talking was over. "Isaiah, I intend to cure your need for womanly companionship in a real permanent way."

With that said, Isaiah was trying to draw his gun, and since my gun was already out, I took a quick step to the left as my first bullet rushed toward the big target. I took another step left as I shot into his body again and again. Shots were echoing, but I focused on Isaiah. Isaiah got off at least one or two shots. The first one was close, but it hit the tree behind me when I took that first step. The second was fired into the ground before he fell down dead on his face as his toes were digging into the dirt.

When the shooting was over, I looked to see who was still standing. It seemed weird that there were two who were still standing with their hands over their heads. They must have thrown their guns on the ground when the fighting started. That left four on the ground who would not need a doctor.

"Jamie, come on over here and help tie up these two. Matt, can you come and give me some help with the others?"

"Sure thing!" was all I could say.

With a few quick steps, I rolled Isaiah over and could see that he was dead. So were the other three. Tom was kneeling beside me as we turned him over. I looked at Tom with a question in my eyes.

"You know what, Matt? This man was the worst of the whole lot. He never was bothered at all in killing anyone, anywhere, anytime. Do I miss him as kin? Not in the least. Good riddance is all I can say!"

Tom was looking closely to Isaiah's wounds and had a smirk on his face, "Hey, what's this, Matt? You sure put your shots where you intended. You done and shot off his manly parts. That first one was straight in the heart. He sure should have listened to you."

"I guess I shot where I was looking! He deserved what he got! That was my only concern."

With that, Tom and I both stood and walked over to Ardith where she still sat on the ground. Jamie and I knew that Tom was the one who could get through to Ardith in her situation.

"Are you okay now, Ardith?"

"Yes, now that one and the others are dead. But we must hurry. We cannot take time to rest. We must get back to their last camp north of here. Maybe Helen might still be there. I surely hope so! They split us up back in Missouri. But I knew that Mason and the other group were following behind us for days on end. This bunch is all that was left of our group. These cowards were worthless. They were even scared of their own shadows, but they were hanging together. It was gold that kept them together. Mason had been gone for several days when I heard talking among the gang. He kept Helen with him and his group for a specific reason. I'm sure of that. So now is the time if we can ever catch them."

With that, Tom picked her up and carried her back to our camp while Jamie and I saddled up our horses and prepared to leave camp. Tom left Ardith with Mrs. Parks and Audrey's good care while we headed out for the other camp with directions from Ardith. Mr. Parks stayed to keep an eye on the two men we left tied up.

After a couple of hours, we rode into the other gang's camp. It was a mess, and the three men who had remained were too scared to fire a shot.

But there was no sign of Helen.

"You three better saddle up and head some direction other than west. That means out of the Territory. Perhaps toward Iowa or Illinois or some other place north or east. If we ever see any of you again, you will die on the spot! Get gone now!"

With that said, we returned to the Parks's camp. We dreaded but knew we had to find out what really happened back in our cabin in Tennessee.

"Let me tell you all as simple as I can. After the raid on the cabin, New Madrid was the first place they spent any time and it was there that Mason split up the gang. Mason took Helen and me with one group and headed west in quite a rush. The other group was to take their time and try to stop anyone who had survived and who wanted to find either of us girls. I find it so hard to talk about Momma. She never had a chance when they first hit the cabin. It was awful. Mason kicked in the door and rushed around the room, while Momma was held by one of his men. He was looking for something that would help him know where Papa had buried some gold. He was yelling at Momma the whole time.

He kept saying, "Where is it? Where is it?"

Mason said that he knew that Pa and Tom had hit it good in Colorado but never had the time to bring the gold to Denver City. That was when Momma got up in Mason's face and ordered him to leave. It was Isaiah who then knocked Momma down. Momma was holding little Jenny when Isaiah hit her. He must have hit her with his fist several times while Mason kept looking for what he called an Indian rattle or some such thing. Mason finally came to himself and saw what Isaiah was doing, and he thought that Momma was dead."

"He became so angry he was going to shoot Isaiah dead, but Tobe grabbed his gun arm and threw off his aim. The shot he intended for Isaiah actually did hit Momma and then Jenny. During all this going on in the cabin, the others tied our hands and had us on their horses. We never had a chance to grieve for Momma, Jenny, or you, boys. With Mason's order, they rode away like the devil was after them. From what I could tell, most of his gang were members or friends of Quantrill's and Tillman's gangs. They were the worst of the worst during the war. We had heard of both groups when we were in town back home!"

Ardith had to stop to get her breath and took a drink of water, then she started again. "Early after the war, Mason and Lane had created a hideout in the Indian Territory. He was always talking about the time it would take to get to that hideout. Every night they were always talking about this gold."

"I don't recall hearing Pa mentioning any gold. I surely did not hear of a map or anything else that would lead them to any gold. But they kept us because they thought we knew more and were lying for Pa and about the gold."

After a few moments, Ardith looked at Tom. "I remember you, Tom. You have changed a lot since that last visit." Ardith then turned to me and asked, "Can you tell me what has been going on, Matt?"

It took a few minutes to fill in the gaps of what Ardith knew and what had happened to us since the raid back in Tennessee. She got all upset hearing about Jamie being hurt and all, but she was so glad Jamie was fine now.

Jamie had to show her the scar on his arm, but as far as the story of the gold, I let Tom fill in those blanks.

Mrs. Parks had brought Ardith a blanket to wrap in to keep the cold away. Soon she was tuckered out, and we were all ready to go to sleep ourselves.

But one thing was certain. Whatever they had done to Ardith had not broken her spirit. She was still so angry that she wanted to dig up Isaiah, shoot him a few more times and then bury him again. We left them all in a shallow grave. That was all they deserved.

The one thing that stayed with me was that she had prayed every day. She had prayed that those who had abused her and Helen would receive their just rewards and now they had. With Ardith back with us I could sleep just a bit better.

Chapter 16

After all this commotion, we decided that it might be best to move our camp to a new location. We could put some time as well as distance between the outlaw gang and ourselves. That seemed the best idea. With that in mind, everyone got up early and started packing things up. That was the fastest and quietest job we had done during our traveling with the Parks.

Tom made Ardith a place in the back of our wagon where she could lie down and hopefully recover from the physical hurts she had suffered. We all knew that only time and love would erase the mental anguish she had endured. To protect her against the cold, Tom wrapped her in a cocoon of blankets. Once she was settled down in the wagon, she promptly fell into a deep sleep that lasted for two days. During that time, she only awoke long enough for nature's call and went right back to sleep. Every so often, Tom took time to check on her.

On the morning of the third day, she was up and about, helping with the meals and whatever needed to be done. Ardith refused to be pampered any longer. She decided that it was her job to drive the mules. That gave her time to rehash the journey from the cabin to Indian Territory with one of us sitting with her or riding our saddle horses along the wagon on the trail. Hearing her story just reminded Jamie and me of our own emotions once again.

Later in the day, Mrs. Parks remarked that we should let her rest as much as possible. She believed that during sleep, a person's body began to repair the damage that had occurred. Most of the time, she believes that sleep, warm food, and having family around always helped a person heal. Medicine and a doctor were only needed when major damage had occurred.

Several days later, Jamie and I found ourselves riding together and we started talking about Ardith, Helen, and Pa.

"She's been hard used, Matt. You reckon she's gonna be all right?"

Tom rode up just as we had started talking. His statement seemed deeply felt.

"She will be, if I have any say so! I am resolved to make things for Ardith better or die trying." And that was all to be said.

We pushed on late every night. Finally, we arrived at Brand's ranch on the east bank of the Verdigris River at about midnight two days later. We had driven hard, knowing that the ranch was too close to spend another night on the trail. Even at that hour, there was plenty of folks up and around to help us. In just a short time everyone was bedded down for a few hours of well-deserved sleep.

It was only after Jamie and I were in real beds with a corn husk tick and a down quilt to warm us that I realized the date. It was only a few days until Thanksgiving and a month until Christmas. A lot of water had run under the bridge since that day back in April. Tennessee and the old cabin would never be the same. Now it was owned by someone else, and that was just fine and dandy with me. I could not imagine what could get me back there. Not now! Not ever! Home was now wherever I laid my head down. There were graves back there, but the new owners promised to care for them. I'd remember them when they were alive, not being dead.

It was hard to imagine how much Jamie and I had grown. During the past months, we had been shot at, wounded, and left with scars on the outside and deep within. Yet we also knew that we had survived, and we would continue on living with the good Lord's help.

Death had been riding along with us on this trail. We had dealt death to those who had killed Mother and little Jenny. They were the same ones who had left Jamie left for dead. They had taken Ardith and Helen and used them horribly. Now we had Ardith back, but we still need to find Pa and Helen.

There were also two questions that had to be answered. One, what to do with Ardith while the three of us continued looking for Pa and Helen. Number two was almost as important. Where would we begin looking?

Time went on and a week was gone. The Parks family had settled into a normal routine with the Brand family and the hired hands. Thanksgiving was a lazy day except for the women. What a meal for everyone.

Tom, Jamie, and I just started giving a hand wherever we were needed. Mr. Brand was an old mossy bull of the woods. He spent time helping Mr. Parks learn the ranch and how to work it. For Jamie and me it was a big ranch. It was about the size of two counties back in Tennessee. The part away from the river had plenty of grass for cows and horses, while the river bottom and along the creeks had some of the best deep dirt for growing crops. The plan was for Mr. Parks to get a crew planting corn, cutting hay, and maybe see how cotton would work come spring.

Riding down along the river bottom made me a believer in this land. The big pecan trees had some of the best nuts found anywhere. Jamie and I had spent an hour and filled two potato sacks full.

After, Mrs. Parks's response was classic.

"Use some time to crack and shell those nuts and a sweet pecan pie will follow! Any takers?" That was a job Jamie and I enjoyed. But the reward was so good and sweet, my oh my!

Mr. Brand's Cherokee wife and her relatives had provided him with claims to a large area of mixed range. There was grassland enough for cattle and horses, and the bottomland would provide soil for food crops such as beans, corn, and maize. This was prime land, and the hope was that cotton would do well also. The nuts from the hickory and pecan trees would help to stretch the food supply in wintertime.

All in all, it was a beautiful land. It reminded me some of back home in Tennessee, and yet it was different in its own way. That difference was soon to make itself known. We were soon to learn that it could go from mild winter weather to a raging blizzard in just a few hours. It could go from sunshine to rain in minutes.

"Tom, you reckon this weather is going to hold?"

"Nope. You can count on it changing, Jamie. Whatever you are looking for, it will change to what you don't want in a hurry. This storm coming at us right now looks like a real twister. Christmas is coming soon. Maybe it won't hit so hard to shut us in. Brand's family thinks that we need to plan to be indoors when it hits. Just stay close by. Hear?"

"That'd sure be nice. I like the idea of being here for Christmas" was all I could say.

Tom and Jamie looked at me like I was somewhere else. They were talking storms, and I was thinking about a present. A nice present for Audrey. The trading post was the only place close for any good choices for a present for a young lady. I wanted this present to be very special. In a few weeks I would be gone, and I wanted her to not forget me or the present. I wanted this to be a holiday that she would never forget.

Meantime our plans had not changed since Audrey and I had spoken on the trail. Tom, Jamie, and I still planned to head out west and find something of Pa's trail before Mason and his gang would find him, if they hadn't already. Helen was still a major part of our searching, along with Pa. Finding Mason meant we would find Helen! Above all else, we must be very, very careful.

Tom kept reminding us of cold camps, snow, rain, heat, dust, and very long days in the saddle. Every conversation we had always led us to the major points we needed to learn. It would be tough. No doubt about it! We wanted Tom to know that he could depend on us to stay the course.

"We're with you regardless what we have to face, Tom. You know that." I constantly told him.

The big storm didn't happen. It ended up being light rain and wind, followed by several cold but sunny days leading up to Christmas.

During Christmas, we all had a great time. It was a great time for Brand's and Parks's families, and we were treated just like family.

It was what Christmas was all about. Singing and games and a big meal were a big part of the holiday. Mr. Parks had been an elder of the church back in Pennsylvania, so it fell to him to read from the Good Book about why we were having a holiday at that time of the year. We all held hands and thanked the Lord for reminding us of what life was all about.

For Jamie and me, it was very special. Back in Tennessee, we had been too poor to buy presents or such. Whenever Pa was gone, Ma was the one who read the stories from the Bible, especially about Jesus's birth. It wasn't much for us. We never heard any preaching back home, but we did know right from wrong. We knew what honor and friendship were about. We also knew how bad it was to lie, for both the liar and those being lied to. We knew that telling the truth might cause some pain, but when all was said and done, it was always better to tell the truth. Lies could come back and bite everyone involved, just like a snake biting the person in the hind end.

Jamie and I had more than once talked about the future with Tom and Ardith. During those times, Tom looked to me like he had a fever or was feeling bad the way he would look at Ardith. Whatever he had, he needed to get over it soon.

"Hey, Tom? Let's you and me head for the trading post. We need some personal items, and the ranch needs some supplies, so we'll just volunteer to go. Sounds like a plan doesn't it?"

Everybody agreed, so we ended up driving the wagon. We needed that much stuff.

Only a week before, we had all gone to the trading post, and I had seen Audrey secretly admiring a brooch under the glass cabinet on the bar at the back. Audrey's Pa had observed what she was looking at and thought he would buy it for her, but it was just too much money for his wallet. Now for me, money was not a problem because we had swapped all the extra firearms and such, and my share was more than enough for the brooch and a few small items for those I cared for. I bought a pocket jackknife for Jamie and a new hatband for Tom. I had thought of a pocket watch but then I realized, who would know what time to set it to. The sun still moved from east to west, and when it was straight up it was noon. That would be good enough for us. I also knew that Ardith needed some fabric to make some new dresses for herself, so I splurged and bought several bolts of fabric. Between Ardith and Mrs. Parks, they were like kids in a candy store, getting an early present.

Christmas morning was bright and cold but also a memorable day as we each opened presents. Audrey just looked at me with big tears forming in her eyes as she admired the brooch. With a shaking hand, she clasped the brooch to the neckband of her blouse.

"Matt, it's so beautiful. How did you ever guess? I've seen this brooch at Mr. Choteau's since that first week we arrived here. I have wished so many times that it could be mine! This is so special. Every time I hold it or see it, it will always remind me of you!"

With that, she stood on her tippy-toes and gave me a kiss on my cheek. I really wanted to kiss her back, but I did not want anyone to think I was that forward.

The best I could do was a quiet "You are welcome!" Then I squeezed her hands together.

Audrey's present for me was a brand-new silk neck scarf, while Jamie and Tom had gone together to give me a new hunting knife. It was one of those Arkansas toothpicks. It was quite similar to the James Black knife that Colonel Bowie made famous before he died at the Alamo. Now that bowie knife was quite a knife. Because Tom was a good hand at the forge, he had added some extra features that would come in handy. He had seen knives like the one he made for me while in the army. With those ideas in mind, he added a serrated edge to the back of the blade that ran three inches from the hilt to the point, and they were for cutting and catching other blades. To that he had added a cutting edge to the backside of the point so that it would cut both going and coming. It was an awesome weapon for killing or whatever it was needed for.

"Hand me your right boot, Matt!"

Following orders, I sat and yanked off my boot and handed it to Tom. He had also prepared a scabbard that he proceeded to sew into the top of my right boot.

"This," he said, "would make for a handy place to keep that sticker."

He had worked hard to make it special just for me. He had balanced it perfectly for throwing if it was ever needed in that way.

Finally, Mr. and Mrs. Parks gave Jamie and me each new winter coats. These coats were something special. They were twill on the outside to cut the wind, while the collar and cuffs were reinforced with bull hide and trimmed with wolverine fur, which they told us would not collect ice or snow during winter weather. The rest of the jacket was lined with sheep wool for comfort and warmth. With gifts like these, we would never forget this Christmas.

It was good to have a party this time of the year. It was to be quite a while before we'd have the chance to be with friends and family in just that way. Just how long was anyone's guess. I, for one, did not want to spend too much time dwelling on this dreary subject.

As Tom was all too frequently stating, "It will just take some time. Time!"

Chapter 17

Days and weeks went rolling past after the three of us had left Brand's ranch. For me, I knew that I was in a real predicament. I was wounded and surrounded by an unknown number of enemies. But I was just trying to survive. Lying there, I let my mind roll back to the journey that brought me to this pickle of a fix.

I remember well the place where the three of us had camped on the Arkansas River back in Kansas. It was after we had left the Parks's place on the Brand ranch in the Indian Territory. After much talking over many days, it was decided that we would split up and continue our searching in two different directions. Tom and Jamie would take the dry route to Santa Fe. My way was to head for the Colorado mountains. Once I was at a place on the map Tom had drawn, I was to head south and then west. My job was not to find the mine but to help find Pa.

"Do you reckon Pa would be at Santa Fe?"

"Well, Matt, it's as good a place as any to start looking! That's for sure. We haven't heard any news from anywhere else!"

Jamie was still confused as to why we had to separate.

"Well, it might be some confusing, Jamie, but what if he was in trouble in one place or the other. If he is in Colorado, then he will have Matt. But if he is in New Mexico then he will have us. The only way to cover both places is to split up. I hate to do that, but it's the only way to do two things at one time."

Tom turned to face me, seeing my blank face.

"You're mighty quiet, Matt. What's on your mind?"

"I agree fully with what you said. We got to split up. It's obvious to me that you and Jamie can get to Santa Fe and look for some word on Pa or Helen. Me, I'll just mosey on straight west toward the San Juan mountains and see what happens. We should give ourselves a certain amount of time, say four or five months or less, and then meet up at a specific place like Taos or Santa Fe. I think that I can handle whatever comes toward me. I just need to look backward so's none of Mason's boys catch me unprepared."

"You're thinking just like I am, Matt. I figure we ought to try and meet back up at Taos or Santa Fe. It's middle of March, so let's get together no later than the first of September. That will give us six months to wander around and hopefully locate your pa and Helen. If you do find yourself into trouble, get word back to us in either place and we'll hightail it for wherever you might be. Just be careful who you trust."

At Fort Dodge, we bought all the provisions we needed. Since I was splitting away from Tom and Jamie, Tom laid what I would need aside then repacked the rest. What I would be needing was strapped on the mule we had bought off Brand's. One thing we all knew was we needed plenty of ammo for our weapons. That was why that mule was so useful. We all had to be ready. We had already had a few gunfights, and we could count that more would be coming. We just did not know when or where.

Water was an important item also. With that in mind, I bought two more canteens. That gave me three, one on my saddle and the other two on the mule. Tom and Jamie had a water keg on their wagon, which satisfied them, along with their canteens. The last thing that I purchased was a spare handgun that I loaded and shoved behind my belt with the handle facing for a left draw. I felt that it would come in handy before too much time passed.

With morning, it was time to head out. Saying goodbyes was always difficult for me. So I just said adios, and with a wave, I headed west out of Dodge. If everything went right for us, we would meet again sooner than later. With the sunrise warming my back, I headed toward whatever trouble might lay ahead.

But like all things, it just didn't happen as nicely as we would like for them to be. I had only traveled three days from our split when trouble reared its ugly head. I was sure glad this old adobe cabin was handy when I needed it. The night before, I had tethered the mule and my horse behind the cabin while I spread my bed inside on the dirt floor. I slept out the night, but the next morning was a different situation.

The sun was just breaking out to the east and I had just finished packing the mule and saddled my horse when this new bunch of yahoos came riding in. They surely weren't expecting to see me any more than I expected them. But I was always ready than most. I was the first one to get off a shot, and the one leading the bunch got his ticket punched for hell. His dying gave me just enough time to dash back into the adobe and slam the door shut. A quick step to my right put me up next to the window. I banged off two or three quick shots, so they knew I was still alive and kicking. I knew without looking that one or two of this bad bunch had got lucky and nicked me in the leg and the side.

All morning long, I kept hearing the roar of a buffalo rifle. Whoever was doing the shooting was forcing me to keep my head down and keeping the water I had just out of reach. I knew that I wouldn't die from the two minor wounds, but without water, it could get interesting soon.

The wound on my side was just a scratch, but the other one was a groove on the outside my left leg just above the knee. I hated having to use that new silk scarf that Red had given me, but it surely worked fine to stop the bleeding.

The old adobe cabin was just one room with half of its roof off and the windows were empty shells. The front door was hanging from one hinge and was stuck partly open. I could see out, but the hombres trying to kill me could also see in the same way. I had been moving around, hoping to be safe from any ricocheting bullets bouncing off the brick-hard walls.

Those two dead outlaws were still lying there in the bright sun. They had been there most of the day. That second one had been way too brave and tried to rush the door. None of the others were brave enough to even try to drag the dead ones out of the way.

They had made the rules, and I was playing by them. If anyone showed a finger or toe, I planned to shoot them off. Because of my shooting, no one else had tried to rush the cabin. They just kept firing often enough to keep me inside the cabin. I just hoped that the horse and mule were still okay behind the cabin.

As for me, my wounds needed better attention to avoid infection, but it would just have to wait until the present situation improved. I was looking for a way to get away and not leave this bunch riding on my trail. As the day dragged on, my leg was starting to talk to me, but I had been hurt worse. The leg had finally stopped bleeding, so I figured it was time to change this situation somehow.

The sun was starting to settle in the west, and night was going to come soon. I started thinking of a way to get away. I looked around the room to see what was available. My glance finally went to the back wall and gave it my whole attention.

I learned the hard way how this all happened. Mostly, it was because I had let my guard down and was not as alert as I should have been. This crazy bunch saw me as soon as I saw them. Their problem was that they had waited to pull their guns until the leader had to say howdy. I could still hear the oily voice of the Mexican leader of the group.

"We been looking for you, amigo. It is time for you to die, yes?"

But before his last words were done, I grabbed for my pistol and took the time to kill the leader while taking a quick dash for the cabin. Thankfully for me, this bunch in front couldn't shoot straight, and the ones in the back could not shoot without shooting some of their own people.

My answer for the leader was a slug right through his belly. In his case, he'd not be troubling anyone ever again. That was a fact. The other man who was about ten feet from the leader was taking a little more time in dying. Toward the end, he kept calling for help, but none ever came from this cowardly bunch.

As I lay there, another Mexican who must been second in command decided to have a conversation. He was on the other side of the clearing behind a wide tree.

"Hey, senor. Do you know the way to Santa Fe? My friends and I have somehow gotten lost. Perhaps you could help us with some directions, *si*?"

For me, I knew he was trying to distract me while they tried again to rush me. This one talking must have not seen Duke and the mule, Clyde.

I had decided to name the mule Clyde since he listened while I talked on the trail. Clyde was a right smart mule. He was so smart that he knew not to argue with me. He had been trained by others, and I had learned what things got Clyde moving.

My response was the best I could come up with. "I think that you don't need any directions on how to get to hell because you already have a couple of compadres who have gone before you."

While I was talking, I had been looking over the back wall again. Then I saw what I hoped would work for me to get out of the fix I was in. The floor down low looked like it had a hump near the corner.

I crawled over to the corner and started to use my bowie knife on the ground. Every few minutes, I kept taking a quick look through the side of the door for anyone trying to sneak up on me. That was when my knife started scraping on a rock. I felt along its sides and realized that it was only a little bigger than my fist, but it was a start on getting out. I quickly pulled the next two blocks that were bigger than the first one.

I eased back up to the door and prepared to fire. I had seen part of a red shirt I'd seen earlier. In the blink of an eye, I saw that red and fired. Whoever it was gave a scream and then the sound of heels were beating on the ground and then a final gasp of air. There was only silence.

"That's one less to feed tonight, amigo! How many are left? I think I can wait you out. Hope you and the rest are nice and comfy!"

Quickly, I was back to the wall and pulled out another rock, which had to be part of the foundation under the wall. The next rock was bigger than the others, and I pulled it loose. I could see that the hole was more than big enough for me to crawl out. Just as I started to stand up next to the mule, the bandit started talking.

"Senor, I think we will be leaving now. There are only three of us left and the money for killing you is not enough for us all to die for. The boss man said you were just a youngster. You would be easy to kill. Me, I think he lied. Me, I think I have heard of you and the younger brother. Word was that you alone killed at least three or four men in fights in Missouri and Arkansas. Yes? Can you hear me? Me and my amigos will leave now. Adios, amigo."

In a few minutes, it sounded like the horses were trotting away. But I wasn't buying it, not for a second. I sure hoped that there was no one crawling around to come at the horse and mule. I was amazed they had waited this long for them.

I went back into the cabin up to the front window and let my rifle enter the opening and waited to see if there was a shot. No bullet came from their guns. With that, I took my hat and held it on my rifle barrel and let it show in the window. That brought out the result I had figured would happen. Three shots rang out, and my hat went sailing across the room. With no time to spare, I grabbed the hat and my bags and skinned out the hole in the back wall. No shot happened, so I gathered the reins of my horse and old Clyde. I could have left right then, but I surely did not want those three or however many there were to follow me after this. At this point, my patience was all gone dry, and my leg was hurting.

I dropped the reins again and stood at the corner of the shack and made out a loud groan.

"Ooh. No, no, no!" With that noise, I hoped they thought I was hit bad. They were in for a surprise.

I could hear the feet of the outlaws running up to the cabin door. I stepped around the corner and took two steps to the door right behind them. They had all gone into the cabin when I said, "Howdy, boys."

With that said, I just started shooting. They were bottled up and didn't even have a chance. Only a few seconds of shooting, and then all was silent. As I walked close to the window opening, I could hear one still breathing barely.

"Aye, I am dying. I… I should have left when I had the chance. Will you help me, gringo, please?"

If he thought I was that green, he was wrong. I just took a quick step to the window and took a quick look. He was waiting for me as I guessed. He fired but was way too quick and missed. I didn't.

The other two were dead, and this one was joining them soon enough. Without a care, I turned my back to the bloody cabin and went back to my horse and Clyde. It took me twice to get in the saddle, but I managed, and with that, I headed west.

I only traveled west for a couple of hours. I knew that I could not go another minute more. With what energy I had left, I stripped the saddle from my horse and Clyde's pack. I then took my blanket and saddle close to the small fire I pulled together. I pulled a long drink from the canteen and then used a clean rag to clean my wounds and put some of the ointment that Tom had sent along for just this situation. After doing all I could do, I just fell asleep without even eating. The one thing I did do though was make sure that my rifle and handguns were loaded and ready to hand. I was learning but the hard way.

It was just before sunrise that I awoke feeling hungry and thirsty. I needed water more than anything else. After a long drink, I was able to think back on more of this journey that we started. Mostly, I was thinking about how Tom and Jamie must be doing on their trail southwest to Santa Fe.

Chapter 18

While I was dealing with these difficulties, I wondered what was going on with Jamie and Tom. Hopefully, they were safer and finding Pa or some information that would help with dealing with Mason and his gang.

I was doing some thinking for myself but also for Matt, wherever he was and Tom. I just had no idea what was going to happen. Only God himself would know, and maybe he was looking somewhere else. But we sure needed his help right now for sure!

We had traveled at least two hundred miles after we had left Matt before we got to Santa Fe. The direction we chose was said by most folks to be the crazy way to go. But it could be done. But also, many a person had died trying. Those who had been across Kansas and Indian Territory and New Mexico said that most of this land was called the Great Plains. Most said that God created this windy plain to hold all the rest together. Some even said that the wind blew from Canada going south and that there was nothing between it and the Texas gulf coast but a few trees and there were only a few of those. The wind blowing all the time could get to a man.

The first part of the trip was the area where the Cimarron and the North Canadian rivers had their headwaters. That would provide some water, but very soon we would leave it behind and water would be scarce. The only neighbors that might be found would be the Comanches. This was their land. It had been one tribe of the Comanches that had taken Pa and Tom into their camp years before. They both had been hurt, and the Comanches always admired brave men, and so they took them back to their camp and treated them. That was when Pa got that rattle while being in their camp. When they were better, they had headed west to Colorado. It was after leaving the Comanches that Pa and Tom had found their gold mine in the mountains.

Tom and I made the crossing without too much difficulty. There were three days when we had to travel at night to avoid the heat of the day. It was the second day that we were just getting to stop to rest for the day that things became dangerous. Tom was still on his horse when he caught sight of a party of Indians headed north, away from us. It was sheer luck that we had seen the roving band of Comanches before they had seen us. Only Tom's quick thinking had kept us from any armed confrontation with them. They were a hunting party, hoping for some game. They were more intent on hunting game or we would have been seen sooner.

We stopped the wagon when we saw them. Tom jumped off his horse and walked out to meet the group of braves. Thankfully, he recognized two of the braves, so he took the chance to talk with his hands empty, the right hand raised open to them. The young braves talked with Tom until they came to an end. The outcome was he gave the braves most of the sugar we had, along with some trinkets we had bought at Fort Dodge. One of the braves had an extra tomahawk that he traded to Tom for a smoking pipe.

During Tom's talking with them about conditions ahead, they gave him a better understanding of what we still had to face. The braves told Tom of where there were at least two small water holes. They knew that in a few more days, these would be gone, totally dried up.

Trouble with people didn't really begin until we arrived in Las Vegas, New Mexico. Las Vegas was a small hamlet about fifty miles north and east of Santa Fe. We figured this was a good place to start asking questions about Pa and Helen.

We drove up to the local mercantile and climbed down at the same time. It was here we could get the needed supplies. Maybe we could get some information about Pa and Helen, hopefully.

It was a rough-looking crowd of folks. There seemed to be ten or twelve of them standing on the boardwalk under the awning of the saloon. They had all been drinking and carousing about when we pulled up. They were shooting plenty of ugly looks directed toward us as we tied the horses to a post.

As we stepped away from the wagon, a crazy, wild, and wooly character burst from the swinging doors of the saloon. With a whoop like some wild Indian, he fell on top of Tom, dragging him down into the dust of the street. It was really hard to tell if the two of them were fighting or perhaps were long-lost relatives.

After all the dust had settled, I could see that they were both laughing. They both acted like two fools as they sat there in the dust and dirt, laughing like children did at a party. As they stood, they were beating each other on the back like long-lost brothers. But this demon man didn't look anything like Tom, so I figured that they were not related. This old fella was at least a foot shorter than Tom's six foot two and probably weighed one fifty if you subtracted the dirty buffalo hide coat. The one thing that kept my attention was the poor fella's head. Most men had some hair on their heads, depending on age and all. But not this man! There was not one hair on his head. What he did have was the ugliest head you could look up on. There were scars on his head that looked like burns that went from front to back. It looked like someone had used a running iron on his head. It was downright ugly!

Tom noticed where my attention was and stood quickly to introduce me to this stranger. He apparently was not a stranger to Tom.

"Jamie, let me introduce you to an ole friend from our last trip out west. This here is Rufus Alonzo Sheffield. Most everyone just calls him Rufus. He's been out west so long that he doesn't know how old he is or what year it is."

"Glad to make your acquaintance, Jamie, lad. Before you die of curiosity, let me explain about this here head of mine. The simplest answer is that I made one too many trips across Comanche land and they come real close to taking more than my scalp. Not too many men get to live to tell about being scalped. One of the fellas in my group used some yarn and a branding iron to put my scalp back together. It hurt something awful, but it was better than dying. That is the reason why there is no hair on my noggin!"

"Well, I'll not let it bother me" was all I could say.

He and Tom began to walk away from the wagon and on to the walkway in front of the mercantile. "I forgot to tell you, Tom, boy. There's a large welcoming committee heading this way. That's all they been talking about. They allowed that they aim to kill you and the boy permanent like." He said this under his breath so that only Tom and I could hear.

"You got your long gun, Jamie?"

I just nodded my head as I jacked a shell into the breach. Tom looked to Rufus and gave him a nod and a wink, and with his left hand, he pulled his gun from behind his belt and cocked it. He left his holstered gun so all could see it but left his hand and gun behind his left hip.

"I do believe that we are ready for them. Let's see just how salty they are. You with us, Rufus?"

"Ain't I always ready? Let them come!"

We then spread apart on the boardwalk as the group of men stopped in the street. It was more of the kind we had seen all along the trail from Tennessee to New Mexico. This was just one more group to deal with.

"How you aim to handle this, Tom?"

"You and the boy fade off to the left and spread out so's they can't get us all in a group."

"It's your call, Tom. We're with you!"

The gang's intentions were obvious. Many were standing with their hands on the butts of their revolvers. The leader of the group was a surly brute of a man. He stood well over six and a half feet tall and weighed three hundred pounds or more. He also had the belligerent attitude of one who usually got his way because of his size and strength. Yet the moment he locked eyes with Tom, he seemed to squirm under his intense stare as they stood facing each other with only fifteen feet separating the two groups.

"Well, if it isn't Bully Welton. I thought that the last whipping I gave you would have taught you a lesson. Seems you are in for another beating. This time, it will be permanent if you try to pull that hogleg!"

"You ain't scaring me none, Wilson! I haven't seen none of your graveyards yet!" Maybe listening to his own talking would give him enough courage to do something stupid.

"Bully, you had better tell that man in the back that if he continues to draw his gun for a sneak shot, you'll be dead first and he'll be second!"

"How you figure to do that when you ain't even got your gun out. You never saw the day you could beat a deck stacked like this one. You got no chance to walk away from this fracas. We intend to bury you and the boy on boot hill. Right, boys?"

They all yelled together. Maybe they needed that to screw down their courage to face our guns.

"You're worth more to us dead than alive, Wilson. You and the boy are gonna die right here and this ole man with you if he tries to take a hand. We'll make it as quick and painless as a bullet in the head can be!"

I heard a clear voice speaking up from behind us.

"Just let it get started, Tom. I'm right here with the equalizer."

It was no one that I could remember. I wasn't about to turn my head to see who it might be, but I could see that Tom knew who had spoken. Those words had an immediate impact.

That last word seemed to be the signal, and the shooting started. Tom took a step to his left and drew his holstered gun while his left gun was already firing. While doing that, he dropped on his left knee as he fired both guns. Rufus had two Remington Frontier .44s out and was firing just as fast as Tom was firing. Since I had stepped behind the water barrel, I just laid my rifle on the rim and shot into the crowd right that were right in front of me. I got off two shots, and then it was all over.

As the smoke began to clear, I could see the carnage that was left on the street. Bully and his crowd had made a fatal mistake by bunching themselves up behind Bully and the two who had stood with him in front of the rest. I could see that there were at least eight men down. Best I could see was that there were six dead or dying in front of us and there were two more who were wounded. My first thought was that at least two others had run off, but that was a mistake. The two who had tried to get to their horses had landed on their faces, dead as they could be. That must have been the elderly stranger with the shotgun. Come to find out, he was another of Pa and Tom's western friends.

It was good for us since the dead ones would have headed to the main camp. There, they would have told Mason and the rest about us.

Tom stood up but kept watching the street for anyone else looking to get that reward. I could see that his eyes and ears were busy as he calmly poked out the empties and reloaded his revolvers.

"Well, Tom, this seems that Bully bit off more than he could chew. That there empty hole between his eyes won't help his vision none at all" was all Rufus had to say as he walked through the dead bodies.

"Rufus, I'll be danged if I can figure where Mason is getting all this trash to hunt us down. The body count is really starting to mount up!"

It was then that I noticed that Tom was bleeding from a wound on his left arm. The blood was running down his arm and splattering on the ground at his feet. In all the noise, Tom hadn't even noticed his arm until I said something.

"Tom, you're bleeding!"

He looked down at his arm and twisted it around.

"Oh, it's just a scratch. Could you get me a bandage from the wagon, Jamie? You can understand that I don't dare to turn my back on this street."

I was already running down the boardwalk and was in the pack with the bandage supplies in a jiffy. I walked over to Tom and Rufus and watched as Rufus bandaged Tom's arm.

Tom was right that it was just a bloody scratch that ran from his upper arm to the shoulder. After that was done, the two of them went to the grisly task of checking the dead bodies that lay in the dusty street.

Tom stopped at the body of Bully Welton. "What a waste" was all he had to say.

It was then that Rufus called for us to join him. He was trying to raise a man up at the back of the crowd.

"This one is still alive, Tom. You want that I should bust him in the head and make him totally dead? The other fella just up and died." They were the two who had stood at the back of the group but had their guns out but not fired.

"Not just yet, Rufus. Let's see if we can get him to talk. Maybe he can fill in some gaps in this story. Mason must be offering some good money on our heads. Let's get him up on the boardwalk and plug his holes."

Some of the townsfolk were there to give a hand. They got the gent to the boardwalk. Someone else had gotten the so-called doctor. Someone said he was also the dentist. It only took a few minutes for the doctor to get the wounds from oozing out blood and used a small amount of whiskey to get him awake enough to talk.

"We want some answers to some questions, partner. You give them to us straight, and we'll let you live. If you play the dummy with us, we'll just pull those bandages off and let you bleed to death. Understand?" Tom wanted answers and soon, and did this lowlife begin to talk.

"Mason has about fifty or sixty men left with him at his camp. I heard tell that he had hired about one hundred men total. He then divided them up and left small groups along the trail. He left some in Missouri and then some in Indian Territory, Kansas, Colorado, and here in New Mexico territory. Each was promised a share of the gold once it was found. The men who were able to kill one or more of you were to get a double share of the gold."

"We want to know where Mason is camped right now."

The wounded man started to clam up when Rufus got involved. He grabbed one bandage and was pulling when he said, "These bandages are coming off, and you'll surely bleed to death! Speak up and be quick about it!"

As he pulled on the bandages, the man began to talk again.

"Their camp is down near Santa Rosa."

We knew that was south of Las Vegas, on the road to Fort Sumner. He said that he had seen Helen there several times. He also remembered seeing an older fella being kept locked up in a soddy. He just didn't know who he was. Of course I knew it had to be Pa!

"You got to know this. Not no one is ever allowed around that young lady. Mason was downright deadly about her safety. I knew of at least two men who Mason personally killed for trying to grab her or put their hands on her."

The need for speed was instantly recognized by us all. With one accord, we all headed for our wagon. Tom had saddled up one horse and tied it to the gate of the wagon. It was only a quick trip to the barn for Rufus to get his Missouri mule saddled and was ready to leave. While I was turning the wagon, Tom stopped his horse next to the few people who were seeing to the outlaw. He had passed out and was still lying in the shade.

"If he has any friends among you or anyone who is willing to take care of him, then do it. But make sure he can understand how sincere we are. Let him know what will happen if he's still around this area once he can ride. I personally will shoot him on sight and any of the rest of Mason's gang who live through what we are bringing to them. They killed this young man's mother and baby sister and stole their two older sisters and left him for dead. He's got an older brother, Matt. He will be showing up around here soon, and he's death on wheels with a gun or knife, so it's best for him to find a healthier climate."

Tom turned to Mr. Sanders, who had used his shotgun well.

"Thank you sir! Your help made all the difference!"

"You are very welcome Tom. Give my regards to your father when you see him!"

With that, we headed out of town.

Chapter 19

"Hey, Tom. Looks like someone is dusting out of town. There must have been one who left while the shooting was happening." I could see the cloud of dust clearly in the bright sunlight.

Rufus's response was very clear. "Let's get going ourselves. I don't believe that we can surprise a gang of that size right now. They know we are here. What they don't know is who survived the shooting and where we are headed. We'll give them something to think about.

"You are right, Rufus, but let's take a moment. I don't want them to see us at all. We'll keep that way for two or three days at least. We know about where they are, but they don't know where we are and when we will show up. We'll just mosey up to the hills and stay out of sight for a day or two. We will find us a hidey-hole where we can camp and yet keep an eye on our camp and their camp also. We'll look for the right time to move on them and not endanger Helen."

"Making them wait will sure wear on their nerves. I can think of several more ways to make them as nervous as hell," Rufus said as he chewed on his chaw and spat onto the ground.

Hearing Rufus talk with that look in his eyes even scared me. Just a bit. He was one man I would never want on my trail.

According to Tom, Rufus had forgotten more about the west than three could learn in their lifetimes. He knew how to live off the land and how to stay on living with enemies all around. I'm sure that he knew more ways to make a person scream and get to the truth than an Apache Indian.

We had only ridden a short distance when Rufus drew us to a halt.

"Tom, these jaspers running away got no idea where Mason's camp is located. If that camp is anywhere near Santa Rosa, they should have turned off here and taken this here trail. It would sure make it a shorter trip iffen they knew their way around. What they did was taking the Cimarron trail south and then they must have picked up the wagon trail to Fort Sumner. That trail follows the Pecos River, which would then provide them with water. But that trail takes twice as long. Iffen you gents don't mind it, we will take the shortcut. Now it is some dry but not near as bad as what you been through the last few weeks or more. Just remember, we will get there much sooner than they, and we can spy on them without them knowing it."

"You called it, Rufus. Lead out and we'll follow. We got enough water for two or three more days. Let's just keep our dust down. No use letting them fellers in on our little secret."

For the next two days, we traveled as hard as we dared, pushing our horses. By the time we stopped, I was plumb tired out. I unhooked the wagon from the mule and unsaddled Tom's two mares and staked them all to graze. The one saddle and my butt made it to the ground near the fire, and I just eased down to the ground. The last thing I was thinking of was food. As I fell to sleep, I could hear Tom and Rufus talking by the fire.

"That's a right tough lad you got with you, Tom! What's the story on this business anyway?" With that question, Tom told the story from the beginning to the present situation.

"I can only say that as tough as Jamie is, his brother, Matt, is even tougher. Matt didn't even blink an eye as he faced the last bunch of men. And he is very fast with a handgun. He is probably faster than even me, if I was fair with him. Keep in mind that he is only eighteen years old."

"Now that you mention him, Tom. I do believe that I have heard some talk about him. They been calling him Matt Guns! Some vaqueros rode from up north, and they were swearing that this gunfighter was hell on wheels with a handgun. From what you say, that must fit him to a tee."

116

"Just remember, I have no respect for Mason. What I do feel for him is pity! Particularly if Matt ever gets to him before any of the rest of us do. He has made promises to his mother and his own self to have revenge on Mason and any of his original crew."

As I fell into a deep sleep, those were the last words, along with a silent prayer for Matt, that I remembered. "Be careful, big brother. Stay safe and leave a few of the bad ones for me."

Tom and Rufus were up at first light and had all the animals saddled and the wagon ready by the time I was up. Embarrassed by my tardiness, I quickly readied myself for the trail ahead. A quick bite of food, and we were moving out.

The first thing I noticed was that the small town was a line on the horizon. It would be less than a day's ride to get there. I looked to Tom, and he could read the question without being said.

"Yes, Jamie, we are going to ease around that town. We'll set up camp on a hill covered with trees that should hide us from Mason and his gang and give us a chance to see the lay of the land. There is a slide of rock that we will keep our back to and cut off any back shooters. Rufus says he has camped there many times before. That is why we will go slow and steady and have time to rest up some."

"Best I can see is that Rufus is our joker in the deck. Mason does not know that he is with us. That's why he can go into that town and see what is happening. Does that work with you?"

"That sounds as good idea as any. I'm just reminded of what the wounded man said. If we get too close and confront them, they plan to kill Helen very quickly. That is very disturbing, Tom. So let's keep that in mind?"

In just a few hours, we were past the town and up in the hills. To get to the spot Rufus had for us to camp was not easy, but we finally arrived there. Without his help, we would never have found this place. After we set up camp, Rufus and Tom talked for quite some time before he headed for town.

"Just remember, Rufus, we need some supplies and hopefully some information on Mason and his gang. Anything that you can find would be helpful without sounding too suspect, especially if there has been any sight of Helen. Just you be careful. You know how gold is. It can change many a man's heart. So be sharp."

"Leave it to me, Tom. These guys are babes in the woods when it comes to Injun work. You boys just make yourselves at home. Keep a watchful eye on the road and anyone other than me heading this way. I'll be back before nightfall."

With that said, Rufus headed out of the camp. He rode around the hilltop and found the trail at a different place than where we left it the first time. I could see that he was a wily fox when it came to hiding his trail.

As Rufus was riding away, I remembered a question I wanted to ask of Tom once we were settled down. It was about the shooting back in Las Vegas.

"Back there in town, Tom. Who was the fella who spoke up behind us when we faced that gang. He must have been the gent with the shotgun. At least one or two of the dead ones had a buckshot along with a bullet or two. Who was that?"

"Well, Jamie, that was an old friend. He's someone just like Rufus, only not so loud as Rufus. He was a man who your pa and I helped when it was needed. He was in a bad situation. That happened on our way to Colorado. He was part of a crew pinned down by Arapahos, and we were there to help. His name is William Sanders, Esquire. He's been a gambler, hunter, and lawman. He's a good man when it counts. Simple but truthful. Remember, you can never have too many friends when a gunfight gets started."

It had been over a year and a half since Matt and I had gotten to know Tom. First as a stranger and second as a friend. He still managed to amaze me with the depths of his character. Talking to him reminded me of a statement that Ma had often repeated to us kids and it fit Tom. "Still waters run deep." That was Tom Wilson.

Chapter 20

It was the next morning after the gunfight at the adobe cabin when I considered what to do next. More than a month had passed, and I knew less than I had when I split away from Tom and Jamie. I began to walk around my camp, and it was then that I saw that there were two horses grazing next to my own. They had followed me from the adobe cabin, still saddled. They were unbranded stock, so I decided to keep them as insurance. The gang that I had faced the previous day had been almost more than I could handle. Prudence dictated that the extra horses would come in handy if there were more to face. Me, I was hiding like a thief from those who would kill me without a second notice.

My first concern had to be getting well from the wounds from the last go-around. I was weak as a kitten. I needed to find a place where my enemies could not find me and where I could regain some strength. The problem was that Pa was out there, somewhere, waiting on one of us to find him before it was too late. So I just got to cinch up my belt and carry on. I would have time to get better after this scrap was over. Pa needs my help, and I will not let him down. Not this time.

I knew that Mason and his gang would kill Pa at the drop of a hat. But I must remember, only after they have the gold. Knowing Pa like I do, I know that he would rather die than tell them anything. Not Pa.

I was getting real tired of being shot at, wounded or not. It was time for me to cinch up and get on to finding Pa. He is probably waiting for us to get there to help him. It is time for me to go on the offensive. No quarter is asked for and none given. That was what that bunch of yahoos had said yesterday. Besides I did not have the time or the want to deal with any wounded prisoners. They would be lucky if I took the time to bury any of them. The coyotes and buzzards would have plenty to eat.

I guess I had a real hate for this bunch of worthless scum. Before being done with them, they are going to wish they had never heard of me or heard about my guns.

I put the horses on picket lines and crawled into my blanket and with my saddle as a pillow, fell sound to sleep. I knew that the horses would let me know if anyone was around. Sleep would do wonders for my wounds and the tiredness I felt.

I slept through the afternoon and all the night. By the next morning, I was ready to saddle up and head west. It was a cold breakfast with no coffee, but I was as ready as I could be. I started with the extra mare and gave my stallion some rest. I had unsaddled the gelding and tied to the mule, along with Duke. Getting the saddle on the mare caused a stitch in my side, but I just ignored it. Everything was packed up. After a time or two, I finally got into the saddle. It was time to get on down the road.

I constantly reminded myself to stay alert because Mason's hired killers were determined to kill me. They could try but were going to fail. Me, I planned to live for a long time after all this is over.

I knew it was crazy, but I turned around a small hill and stopped with the horses and the mule. I crawled up to the top of the hill and looked back east at my back trail. Maybe see who was following me. All morning, I had felt that someone was trailing me.

Being careful, I lay down at the bottom of the trees and brush that hid me from anyone on the trail below. Sure enough, there were at least three left over from yesterday's fight at the old cabin.

I slipped down and got back on one of the mares. I walked her to the edge of the trail just as they saw me. I found myself speaking softly but loud enough so they could hear me.

"Well now, fellas. Let's play this game by your own rules!"

With that, I dropped the reins and put the spurs to her. Two leaps and we were on the trail and right in front of them. They were not expecting to see me there for sure. My guns were already out, and so I just started banging shots before they could get to their guns. The two on my right were down and dying, and the one on the left was trying to stay in the saddle and his gun was lying in the dust of the trail. I just sat there, poking out empties and reloaded. Then I dropped to the ground as the last one fell slowly from his horse. As I walked over to see how he was, I knew he was going to die. My first shot had broken his arm and the last shot was into his belly.

"Do you have any folks missing you?"

"Boy, I got nobody. If I did, they wouldn't care much anyway. I'm going to die, ain't I?"

"Yes! You are getting what you earned. It could take a long time. I'd get it done sooner than later iffen I were you. Myself, personally, I don't plan to wait for you to die. You would do the same for me."

I picked up his revolver, rolled the chamber around once, and made sure there was one bullet left in it then left it near his hand.

I turned around and walked back to my horse and climbed on the saddle. This bunch had nothing that I needed, so I just left their things as they lay. Someone would come along soon enough and do what needed to be done.

"Use that last bullet wisely. It could take some time before you die if you don't. The pain could be pretty bad."

The thought running through my mind was about how glad I was that it was him and the rest, not me!

Once I was in the saddle, I looked down the valley. There was dust cloud blowing up off the trail. With that in mind, I got the horses and the mule and headed down the trail. There were more of them coming. Fine with me, so I started looking for a place that would work for an ambush. It was an hour later that I found what I was looking for.

I pulled the horses and the mule off the trail and herded them into a grove of trees around a small hill beside the trail where a creek ran almost dry. I dropped down and pulled my rifle out of the boot and eased around the hill and sat behind a boulder next to the trail. It was only a few minutes later when a group of four came into view. I already had found a good-sized rock that I planned to use in my plan.

When the leader got even with my hideout behind the boulder. I took the rock and hit the leader's horse in the nose with the rock. For once, my throw was on the money, and the horse reared up and fell backward, pinning the rider under the horse. I stepped into the trail and began shooting as fast as I could lever the rifle. Two more horses were down, and the last man was trying to get his horse turned around to run away. I waited just a second and shot him out of the saddle as his horse was running away. I knew where my shots had gone, and none of this bunch would need help anytime soon. Death had come for them that day.

I walked carefully to where the leader was lying on the ground.

"Today is just not your lucky day. That horse is never going to walk again!" With that, I shot the horse in the head. Then I walked around the dead horse to get a closer look at the leader of this bunch, while giving his gun a kick.

"You are in a mess of trouble, amigo. Know what I mean? I'm guessing that you got a broken leg under the horse, and that saddle horn didn't do your ribs any good at all. Now I could help you out, but I'm doing nothing to help you until I get some questions answered. Understand?"

"Listen, boy, I'm hurting some terrible. I could use some water?"

"After my questions!"

"Damn Mason, he sure lied to us when he sent us to find and kill you and the others. You been a handful all by yourself, boy. Ahh, my leg!"

"Question one. Where is Mason and the rest of his gang?"

"Why should I lie now? They're down in New Mexico near Santa Fe or Taos. Ah, some water, please?"

I gave him a small sip and stepped back.

"Question two. Where is my pa and my other sister?"

"The girl is with Mason. I saw her myself. The last I heard, your pa is somewhere across the border in southwest Colorado. Maybe Mason has him now too. Can I have another drink before you kill me?"

"Here's a drink. Too bad I don't plan on killing you like this. But you will wish I had killed you before your end comes!"

With that, I took my rope and dropped a loop over the horn of his saddle and tallied the rope on my saddle horn. I grabbed the mare's reins and led her to pull that horse off the outlaw. In just a few seconds, it was done. I rolled up my rope and put it back on my saddle.

The outlaw had fainted away when the horse's weight came off his leg. I splashed water on his face and brought him back.

"Partner, you are in a bad way. Here's your canteen. Your pistol is right over your right shoulder. If I were you, use the gun wisely. I gave the same deal to one of your friends a few hours ago."

"Yeh, I saw him and his group were all dead as we rode by them."

"Listen up. If there are anymore of Mason's men who find you, they will probably shoot you and save the time and trouble to deal with your wounds. If you do live long enough, maybe some Christian folks might help you out. If you do see any of your group, give them a message from me. Tell them all that I done declared war on the lot of you. No quarter. Remember that. Not a one of you are safe until I'm dead or Mason and all his gang are dead and gone. Remember that!"

With that, I gathered the horses and the mule and headed west. I turned back to make one last statement.

"If you do live long enough, tell them all that I will be riding for them all. Those who had anything to do with my mother and baby sister being killed, the ones who almost killed my younger brother and took my sisters for slaves back in Tennessee, are the ones I want. I want that message to get back to Mason and those responsible. If it wasn't for that one thing, I would shoot you now so you could join the others lying here dead. If you do live and I see you on any street or any saloon, I will kill you or any of the rest without a thought. Understand that? If you see me, then you better find a different place to be or you will die!"

As I rode away, I could hear the feeble voice of the outlaw begging me to help him. Me, I just had better things to do. Time was a-wasting.

Chapter 21

As I sat leaning against a tree three days later, it came to me. I was going to find me one of that original gang, the ones that hit our home. With just one of them, I could get better answers. That last one had no idea where Pa was or nothing else about Helen. It seemed time to head for a meeting with Tom and Jamie.

With that in mind, I cut loose the one gelding and kept the mare, along with Duke and Clyde. The stallion was worth any three horses, and Clyde was too cranky for anyone else to deal with. He and I got along quite well, thank you, and we headed south.

It was only a few days later that I came up on a small village baking in the sun. There were only half a dozen adobe homes and a cantina. There were two old men sitting under the veranda out of the sun when I stopped and slid out of the saddle. My wounds had improved, but my clothes were getting some ragged.

Keeping my eyes on the door, I used my hat to brush some of the dust from my clothes and loosed the thong from my pistol then pulled it two times to make sure it was loose and ready.

"Food inside, amigos?" was my question to the two old men.

"If you have some dinero, yes. Perhaps tequila to go with it."

"Water is all I need. Tequila might go to my head, gracias."

I just stood and stretched for a moment in the cool air on the veranda, enjoying the quiet time.

"Any other strangers been around recent?"

"There is one Anglo sleeping off his tequila. Yes. He sits in the corner. He smells very badly. He seems to be looking for someone. Could that someone be you, perhaps?"

"I'm guessing it is me he's looking for. Perhaps after I eat, I will awaken him. Maybe he and I can talk things over!"

With that, I walked into the dark saloon. I stood for a second, letting my eyes get used to the dimmed light. I stepped to the bar and ordered some food and took a seat across the room from the sleeping thug. He looked familiar for some reason. Maybe it was because he looked like all the others Mason had hired. He smelled bad, and his clothes were filthy.

It took two plates of beans, steak, and tortillas, along with three glasses of cold water to fill me up. I sat and thought through what I needed to do.

With my mind made up, I pulled my knife with my right hand, my left hand holding my belly gun. It took just a few steps where I could lean over and removed the thug's gun from his holster, then I used my right leg to give him a good shove off the seat.

"What the—" was all he got out when I laid the knife against his neck right under his Adam's apple whilst I sat astraddle him.

"What you have here is a very cranky and unpleasant young man. I have been shot and shot at, and I have killed, at the last count, about twenty of your so-called friends. You are about to become number twenty-one. I'm trying to decide whether to cut your throat and be done or maybe get some answers. Your choice!"

"You got the drop on me. What is it you want from me?"

"Me, I really want you dead, but I need some information before that happens."

With that, I grabbed him by the collar and set him back on his seat. One of the old men was reading my mind, and he showed up with a length of rope, which I used to tie the outlaw to the chair. When I was done, I left his right hand and arm free. I kept a hold of his wrist as I sat across the table from him.

"Let's start with names. You probably know me. I am Matt Allison. So which one of Mason's gang are you?"

ELIJAH BRUNSON

That was when I saw his hat laying on the floor. It was a derby, and he sounded like being from New York. I knew then who he was.

"I know who you are. You must be Tommy Smith, the pervert. Right?"

"Yes. What of it? But I ain't no pervert neither."

Trying to yank his hand away, he yelled, "Heh, stop with that there knife," as I laid my knife over his fingers.

"What it means is you may have one chance and only one to keep all your fingers."

With that, I stabbed my knife between his thumb and index finger, and the knife edge was laying right above the other four fingers. I kept his arm on the table with my left hand.

"Where is Mason and the rest of the gang?"

Tommy did not hesitate with his answer.

"Mason and the gang are camped at the base of Green Horn Mountain."

"Now that was easy, wasn't it? Does Mason still have my sister? Does he know where my pa is?"

With that question, I put a little more pressure on the knife and blood was starting to run from the first finger. Tommy was sweating and bleeding, and if I was not mistaken, he had just peed his pants.

"Mason has them both. Last I knew, your pa wouldn't talk, and Mason was running out of patience with him. That's all that happened before I left the camp."

Tommy was looking right into my eyes. I knew exactly what he saw. He was going to lose his fingers and maybe get his throat cut. That was what he certainly deserved.

"Why are you here and not with the other gang members? Don't lie to me either." I put some pressure on the knife.

"The others gave me two choices. Either leave and never return or die right then and there. Several had accused me of trying to abuse the girl. Mason had told me before not to be bothering her, and I'm more scared of Mason than any of the others. So leaving and living was a better choice."

"So you never tried to abuse my sister? That's a laugh. You had run from the law back East for that very thing. You left those young girls bloody and beaten and more than one had their throats cut. I'm sure you were caught trying to mess with my sister! What you get now is what you have deserved many times over!"

With him looking me straight in the eyes, I leaned on my knife and removed his four fingers just that fast. I sat there for a minute or two and then leaned over and tied a strip around his arm to stop the bleeding.

"We don't want you to bleed out, so let's lay a hot iron on that stump. Maybe a dull knife or ramrod might do the trick to sear the bleeding and the pain."

With that, the bartender used a hot poker to sear the stumps of his fingers. Tommy passed out for several minutes until I spilled a glass of water on his face.

"Unless you are good with your left hand, your gun will be no good to you now. Maybe you can at least use it to shoot yourself. Who knows? I did that much for two of your partners. They both died quicker that way!"

As I untied him from the chair, the cook put a bandage on his stump. With that said, I left his gun across the table next to what was left of his hand.

"Describe my pa for me?"

"As I look at you, you look a lot like your pa. He has the same color hair and eyes. His eyes always look like blue ice, just like yours. Would you please get me some help with this hand? This cook doesn't know what he is doing!"

"Yes, that sounds like Pa," I said as I wiped my blade against his shirt.

"Can he walk and function okay?"

"Well, he's been some beat up. But he could still walk the last time I was there! You got to help me with this hand. I'm still bleeding like a pig. Please?"

The cook removed the bandage from his stump as I went back to the stove and removed the iron to use on the bleeding wounds.

"Stay right still and this will be over very soon," I said as his hand sizzled for the second time from the poker. I gave him one last piece of advice.

"These folks will let you go when I'm gone. They will bandage your hand. When that's done, get on your horse and go anywhere except south, west, or east. That just leaves you north. I plan to leave word in every town I come to about how you lost your fingers and why. No one will ever help you out here in the west. People will not allow anyone who would abuse women, girls, or young children. They usually hang people caught doing any of the kind. I will leave that to others to deal with you in their own way. Goodbye, Tommy. Hell is too good a place for someone like you."

I gathered the lead line of the mule and horses and was dropping into the saddle when Tommy staggered out of the cantina. He had tried to handle his pistol with his left hand. He was trying his best to shoot me. He actually was able to fire twice and missed both times. But I was not going to leave him where he could be on my back trail, one hand or not. With that in mind, I took my time and shot him in the heart, and he was dead before he hit the ground.

I sat there on my horse thinking about what had just happened. First, I thought about torturing him with the knife. No, that didn't cause me any guilt feelings. Second, I ended up shooting him down. I couldn't find a bit of remorse for him, not a bit.

Tommy deserved what he got and more. Death was too good for him. His past just caught up with him. But he wasn't going to live with one hand. To him, there was no future for someone like him. With only one hand, he wanted to die and that was what he got. Death by bullet.

I still had half a day before I planned to stop for the night, so I looped the lead rope around the horn and started to leave the village.

The two old men had never moved and were still sitting on the veranda, and they spoke to me.

"Should we bury him, amigo? We could just leave him out in the prairie for the vultures."

Hearing that, I tossed them a silver dollar.

"He is not worth it, but bury him deep. He will start to stink way too soon if you don't. Adios."

"Vaya con Dios, young warrior!"

I heard them talking as I rode away.

"That is one mean young hombre. His heart is very black with revenge and hatred. I think we should light a candle for him! Perhaps we should place one or more for those who are misfortunate to get in his way."

"Si, si!" was all the other old man had to say.

Chapter 22

While I was headed south to meet them, Tom and Jamie were waiting for Rufus to get back from town. Once he returned, they could begin to talk and plan on how to deal with their problem.

Rufus had gone around the town and came in from the south trail. Hopefully, that would throw off any suspicion. Santa Rosa had just recently been settled by Don Celso Baca, a don from Mexico. He had established himself as one of the local leaders.

Rufus noted that some new buildings were being done along the main street as he headed toward the center of the town. As most western towns, they had two saloons facing each other along with a restaurant and a dry goods store. One saloon was getting most of the business, so that was where Rufus headed.

Swinging through the batwing doors, he took in the customers at a glance. He strode over to the bar and ordered what he wanted.

"Hey, barkeep. Gimme a beer. Man, that sun out there could fry a man's hair right off his head." As he spoke, he pulled his battered hat off his head to reveal his tortured pate to the onlookers. Many gasped with amazement at the sight.

Someone in the back of the bar said in a quiet voice, "Looks like someone done tried to kill you but only carved on your skull."

Rufe's only response was, "Yeh, but he who tried to get my hair got more than he was expecting. I'm still alive, and he has been dead many years now!"

He turned to the barkeep and asked, "Where's this bunch that's offering gold to anyone who can kill some young folks from back East. Someone said that they are so bothersome?"

The barkeep, who was almost as ugly as Rufus and none too pleasant with folks he wasn't acquainted with, replied, "Who's asking?"

"That would me. Rufus Alonzo Sheffield. That's what my ma named me. Most folks just calls me Rufus or Rufe. Them who are younger or I don't like just call me mister, if you get my drift, sonny!"

As he was talking, he had pulled his buffalo-skinning knife from its sheath and began to clean his fingernails. He did that for a few moments before he turned to the barkeep with a malicious grin and stabbed the knife down between the barkeep's fingers as they rested on the bar.

"Now you, sonny, I think I like. You can call me Rufus."

The barkeep was not only ugly but was also crazy mean. Rufus could have gotten on his bad side very quickly. But Rufus realized that the barkeep was ugly but was also some feared of Rufus and his knife. The barkeep looked down and saw a small stream of blood running from his finger, which he wrapped with a bar towel.

"Yes, sir, Mr. Rufus!"

"No, just Rufus is enough. You heard my question the first time. Where are this bunch camped anyway?"

Before the barkeep could have answered, a voice from one of the tables behind him spoke up.

"I can answer your question, stranger. Come on over and have a seat. Barkeep, bring the man a glass of beer. On me."

"Yes, sir, Mr. Lane." The barkeep was quite ready with his response, and I knew why also.

This was no one else than the notorious Mr. Lane. He was commonly referred to by the name Cherokee. This could turn bad quickly, depending on which direction this conversation went.

Lane was one really bad man in the East, West, or any direction you went. He had come out of the Indian Territory just before the war. He stood all of five feet, seven inches and weighed less than one hundred and fifty pounds soaking wet. He was freckle-faced with

stringy reddish-blond hair down to his collar. If he had ever possessed a sane mind, it had been lost when he was a young child. At
the tender age of twelve, he had killed his first man with a butcher
knife. It seemed the man was trying to rape his mother. When the
sheriff got there, he asked Lane why he had killed the man. Lane's
response stayed with the sheriff a long time afterward. He responded,
"The man refused to pay of momma's services. No money, no service.
Nothing is free!"

The sheriff knew that a young boy with that callous attitude
would never turn to anything good. The sheriff was right. Lane
had turned into a stone-cold killer. At some time before the war, he
became a member of Mason's gang and then his second in command.
The war was the justification that all these gangs needed to leave a
bloody path through the South or anywhere else they landed in the
West. Rufus knew he must be very careful with this man or he could
die and that quite suddenly.

"So are you interested in joining up with us?" Lane asked.

"Well, sure. I heard tell that you were paying in solid gold. None
of this paper money. I could sure use some of that. Buffalo hunting
has fell way off. You know a man's got to live, right?"

"Well, there is only one catch to this deal. You got to live to
collect these wages. These young boys we're looking for have been
responsible for killing or wounding over twenty of our men."

He considered the tabletop for a moment.

"We just sent seven of our best men up north to kill the oldest boy. He goes by Matt. Some folks have started calling him Matt
Guns. That's downright funny. But folks say that he is downright fast
with a handgun. Iffen the men of ours don't get him, I may have to
see just how good he really is for myself."

Lane rubbed his chin and finished up. "Anyway, if you want to
join up, our camp is just north out of town over along the river. You
can't miss it. Just make sure that you sing out that I sent you or they'll
gun you down. Understand?"

Rufus knew that he had to be very careful in how he responded.
"I got a couple of pards waiting just outside of town. Soon as I collect
them, we'll amble out that way."

"You do that. More the merrier. We can use men like yourself. Men who have some bark still on the trunk. Most of this bunch we got barely know one end of a gun from the other."

With that said, Lane rose from the table and with five others, headed for the door.

Rufus stood where he could see the six of them as they mounted their horses and headed out of town. The next second, there was a gunshot. It even caused him to pause.

One of Lane's riders had bumped into Lane's horse and Lane almost fell from his horse into the street. Without a moment's hesitation, Lane backhanded the man across the mouth and with the same motion, pulled a gun from his waist and shot the rider through the head, dropping him dead in the street. The racket of the shot brought all conversations to a stop. Lane's comment could be heard by all in the saloon.

"Damn clumsy fool. Should have watched what he was doing!"

With that, Lane and the other riders continued out of town, leaving the dead man lying in the street.

"Man gets real sudden, wouldn't you say?" was all the barkeep had to say.

"Jest a mite. Jest a mite" was all that Rufus would say as he stood and walked out the saloon door.

With his eyes shaded against the glare of the afternoon sun, Rufus watched as Lane and his riders continued out of town. After waiting on the veranda, Rufus went to the mercantile and then mounted his mule and headed out of town the opposite direction. After riding for twenty or thirty minutes, he pulled off the trail and swung behind a small hill where he could look down his back trail.

Seeing no dust or riders heading his way, he saddled up and headed back to where Tom and Jamie would be waiting for him. It was still early afternoon when he arrived back at their camp. It only took a few minutes to share with Tom and Jamie what went on in town and what he had learned.

Tom's reply was quick and to the point!

"Let's get some rest. When it gets dark, we're heading for Mason's camp. Once we get there, we will need some time to find where they are keeping Helen. Then we can come up with a plan to get her out. We need to come up with a plan that will hopefully work and without any of us getting hurt in the process. We must keep Lane and Mason in mind. If we can do this without killing, then we have a chance. Once we have Helen away and safe then we can think about taking care of Mason, Lane, and the rest who were at the cabin back in Tennessee. Jamie, you take first watch, and then wake me up in an hour. We all need to be on our toes for whatever is in store for us tonight."

Rufus was grumbling as he headed for his blankets.

"Lane is one man who needs killing. That man is downright crazy. Needs to be killed, sure enough!" With that, he started to snore.

Jamie was sitting alone on a rock, speaking out loud to himself, "I wonder what is happening with Matt. We could use him big-time."

Chapter 23

With the information from Tommy Smith, I decided it was time to get as close to the outlaw camp as soon as I could. I knew that Jamie and Tom would be needing my help.

It was time to ride.

I headed toward Taos and Green Horn Mountain. Tommy, as bad as he was, had been telling the truth as far as he had known at the time. It had taken me two and a half days to get to a point where I could look over the land and find Mason's camp without being found by any of his outlaws.

It was late in the day when I decided to leave Clyde and the horses to graze. I followed the directions I had picked up and started looking for the trail that would lead me just above Mason's camp. As I lay hidden by a brush next to a large boulder, I had a good view of the campground.

It was just as the sunlight was fading away in the west that I started out hunting. I had just got to a better hiding place without being seen. This place gave me a safe place where I could see into the camp but would not be seen by anyone down below.

"Hey, Lane sent me out to join with the gang!"

It was a lone rider who called out to the guard near the rocks that got my attention. I could see how the camp was situated. Where I sat, I could not be seen from the guard. Sitting there, I could locate how many people there were. That was when I saw the soddy. Tommy had said that was where Pa was kept.

I could hear the guard talking with the new recruit who had just arrived. I was trying real hard to hear their conversation when I heard a woman beating on a pan. I turned and knew I was looking at Helen. She was calling them all to the meal that she and two other women had prepared.

I was preparing to settle down to wait until darkness would arrive. At that moment, I felt that there was someone extremely close by. Without a thought, I pulled the knife from my boot and turned to stick whoever had tried to sneak up on me. But I was stopped by a low voice. "Hey, brother!"

I knew immediately who it was.

"Now, is that any way for a brother to say howdy to his family? And with a big knife like that!"

I knew that voice belonged to Jamie. As I leaned back, I could see that Tom was there with Jamie. What a relief it was to see them both again.

Tom said in a whisper, "I hope that you plan to remove those spurs before you go traipsing down there with the sinners. Jamie and I have some plans already working. Let's just take a few minutes and merge our two plans into one. Then we can rescue Helen and get out of here."

As I finished removing my spurs, I said in a whisper, "Tom, Jamie. I am so glad to see you two. Do you know that Pa is down there? Sitting here, I thought for sure that was Helen. I know for a fact that Pa is down there. Now, if you are saying for sure that's Helen, then let's get them both. I saw her, but I wasn't totally sure it was her."

"Pa's down there, you say?" Jamie was so happy.

"Yes, Pa is in that soddy right down below us. I'm guessing that must have been Helen who's been cooking for that bunch. I have no clue who the other women are."

"Did you notice that last man that just arrived in the camp?"

"Yes" was all I said.

"Well, that man is our joker in the deck. His name is Rufus. That bunch don't know that he is one of us and not one of Mason's gang. Let's watch for a bit and see what happens with your pa and Helen."

As we watched, one of the men filled a plate with food and headed for the soddy. When he got close, we saw there was a guard right by the door and he was holding a Greener, a shortened shotgun that was downright dangerous up close. The two men laughed together as the guard disarmed him before he opened the door, allowing the man to give the food to another man who was inside the door.

"Well that answers several questions. One of us will be the person to get your pa out of the soddy. It must be done as quiet as possible."

"Can you do it, Matt? There are two, but you can handle them, right?"

"I'll get it done!" I felt some dread facing two grown men, but oh well, it was now or never. That was why we got this far.

"So while you're doing that job, Jamie and I, with Rufus's help, will find Helen and get her out of there. We need to be as quiet as we can. Using that big knife should be the way to go, Matt."

"Get your pa out and head up the draw right below us. Your mounts are there with ours also. Get him on a saddle and be prepared for Jamie and me to show up with Helen. Having those two extra horses and saddles sure will come in handy. Let's just take a few more minutes before we open this ball."

With a nod from Jamie, I was as prepared for what was to happen as I could be. I leaned against a boulder and pulled out each pistol and used a tail of my torn shirt to clean them. I pulled all the bullets from both pistols and made sure that they were clean and ready for use, if needed. The last thing I did was to pull my knife and stropped it a few swipes on the heel of my boot.

"I'm as ready as I ever will. How about you, gents? You ready?"

Jamie and Tom both shook their heads, knowing that words were not needed. With that done, I started to ease myself down the ravine that led to the back corner of the soddy. I knew that I would only have just a few seconds to get Pa out and then back up the hill.

Thankfully, all the gang's focus was on the meal that Helen had prepared and Rufus's jokes.

So much had happened to me in the last few weeks and months, but I had no premonitions or fears. Calmness settled over me. I was ready to do what needed to be done. My job was to be quiet but deadly. I could see that what Tom had taught us was going to be very handy.

The gang members were all sitting with their backs to the soddy and were all looking into the fire as they listened to Rufus's story. Being the newest member, the gang were glad to hear his tales rather than listen to each other's gripes.

I took a quick look toward where Tom and Jamie were heading around the camp. Jamie was to stop halfway around and put his rifle on the biggest hombre around the fire. As I saw Jamie taking his spot, I knew it was time for me to get busy doing my job.

I had left my hat hanging on the saddle horn, and Jamie had my spurs. I didn't want a hat to get in the way. As I was stepping forward, I saw a gang member was up and heading toward the soddy. As I stepped back into the shadows, I knew he was the one who had brought Pa's supper. As he got close to the soddy, he pulled his gun from his holster and left it with the guard who had stood and turned his back to me. With just a quick step, I was there with my left hand on his mouth as my right brought the knife into his back and into his heart. While keeping a grip on him, I used him to push him into the other man in the soddy. It was only a quick second and he was dead as well. I took the Greener from the one guard and his pistol. I could see that it was Pa as I handed him the weapons.

"Pa, it's me, Matt. Can you stand and walk?"

"Yes, son, I can. Let's get out of here before they see what has gone on."

With that said, Pa went out first and was around the corner like a shadow. I was just behind him as I pulled the door shut. The last thing I heard as we headed up the ravine was Rufus regaling those around the fire with another one of his stories.

So far, we had managed our part of the plan. Now if only the rest of the plan would work as well.

While Pa and I were climbing the hill, Jamie was keeping his eyes on the campfire where Rufus continued to tell one story after another. Jamie could see Tom as he worked his way through the horse herd and saw where Helen was located. She was sitting with her back to the fire and was looking up toward the stars and whatever was out in the darkness. Luckily, she was looking toward the horse herd. With just a quick wave, Tom got Helen's attention. She saw Tom standing next to two horses that were dark as night. Tom gave her another wave with his hand. Helen was a quick learner.

She stood up and told the other two women that she was going out to answer the call of nature. One gal said, "Don't take too long. You know how crazy these men get. Mason or Lane are the worst!"

"Yes, I do know."

With that said, she took to walking to Tom's left and toward the trees at the base of the hill. With a silent step, Tom was at her side and took her hand.

"Not a word," he whispered as he began to lead her up the mountain toward where Jamie was still sitting. They got to the horses without any noise or disturbance in the camp.

"No one has noticed anything just yet, Tom. But I bet in about ten minutes or less, they are going to miss either Helen or Pa or his very dead guards," Jamie whispered.

"Let's get out of here as quickly as possible then. Helen, no talking. Just follow Jamie. I'll follow in a bit. Matt and your pa will be waiting for us where we left the horses."

It only took the three of them a few minutes to get back to the horses. Pa saw Helen and took a quick step and hugged her to his chest. Me, I spoke off quietly, "Pa, Helen, we got to get on down the road. This bunch are going to be real riled up. Let's be far from here and somewhere we will have some protection."

Tom came running up and leaped on to his horse.

"Let's ride."

Chapter 24

We rode for two hours as I led them back to my camp. I grabbed my gear and packed it all onto Clyde with it all. In just a few minutes, we were riding together. It took just an hour until Tom found the place that we had agreed to meet with Rufus.

Jamie said that he had gotten the most sleep recently, so he would take the first guard duty. The rest of us lay down for a few hours of sleep. Pa and Helen were too tired for any talking. It could wait.

The next morning, Tom, Jamie, and I sat with Pa and Helen and took turns relating all that occurred up to last night. When we told Pa of Ma and baby Jenny, it was clear to me just how hard it was for Pa. He sure had a hard time keeping things together. Jamie and I both knew how Pa and Helen had to feel. Pa stood and walked away from the fire and stood looking into the sky. Finally, he turned back to the fire and listened to the rest of the story. I could see how glad Pa was to know that Ardith was safe back in Indian Territory. He was so happy that she was with the Parks.

As Pa sat down next to me, he started looking me over. I sure wasn't much to look at that time. I was glad that Tom did most of the talking. When Tom finished, we all looked around the fire and closed our eyes for a moment or two.

Pa's first words to me were this. "You've grown up some, Matthew. Much more than I ever expected. I can see that you've suffered some, just like Jamie. I know that you boys and the girls will be marked by this experience. I have to say truthfully that most of this is my fault. If only—"

I quickly stopped him with a hand on his shoulder.

"Pa, life has its problems. This is not your fault any more than anyone else's. If there is any fault, it is those who wanted what they had never worked for and were willing to kill for it. Whoever Mason thinks he is or why him or any of his gang think they deserve anything, they are wrong. We have left their bodies on the trail from Tennessee to New Mexico and many places in between. If they try to keep following us then they can continue dying. They want something for nothing, but they can guess again. The only thing that they are going to get is the fire that comes out of our guns."

"Well, Matt, you sure look and sound like a grown man. Looking at your weapons and the way you dealt with those guards tells me you've made it. Can you use those handguns as good, son?"

"Yes, sir. I had one of the best teachers available excepting you, of course. Tom didn't tell us for a long time who he was. But it all worked out. He just started in teaching everything he knew that would help us to be good men and follow the laws as best as we could. When we got into a gunfight with some of Mason's bunch, Tom got hurt. That was when we learned who Tom was. We should have remembered him, but Jamie and I were both so young that his memory didn't stay with us."

"I always knew that Tom would make it back and would give a hand with what needed to be done."

Pa looked across the fire at Tom. "He's the finest young man I've ever known. He's one you can ride the river with. There isn't too many like him. Rufus is another. I just wish that I could have been there when you needed me the most."

"Well, you are here now. That's what matters. We all agree. Let's get with it and get on a move on, how about it?"

Rufus had played it perfectly. As he made the camp, he was off his mule, and with a quick jump, he reached Pa and gave him a big hug. After a few words with Pa, he attempted to shake Helen's hand. She wouldn't have that, but she gave him a big hug.

"I sure was in a sore spot when you got Helen out of the camp last night. I thought for sure that all the gang were going to shoot me down where I was standing. That was when the fur hit the fan. When you spooked that herd of horses was what saved me. But of all the people, Lane was the one who spoke up for me. He's just crazy as a fox. Lane just told them that I could not have known that any of you boys were around. I'm sure he is still trying to figure out if it was you, Matt, or Tom there who broke your pa out of the soddy. The two dead guards sure couldn't tell what happened. Mason and Lane had talked, and it was Lane who announced that without your pa, there just was not going to be any gold to pay to any of the extra hands. When the outlaws got the horses settled down, they just started leaving the camp. You know me, I just up and said that I was heading for the plains and see if there were any bufflers. They all had heard me say that I was only there for the gold. It was so easy that I almost forgot to watch my back trail."

"I was doing some thinking. I was betting that Lane might have thought I was in on the deal with you folks. So he had me trailed by two yahoos that don't know one end from the other. I shook them off easy enough. I just wandered around with no place to go. Those two gave up real soon. After I lost them, I rushed to join up with you all. So here I am."

After some long talking with Pa, Tom, and Rufus, the decision was to head into a big town. We all wanted to leave a clear message to Mason, Lane, and the rest that remained of the gang what would happened if they showed. We had no plans to deal with prisoners or wounded members of Mason's gang.

Chapter 25

We got to Las Vegas early in the afternoon. Pa and Tom, along with Rufus, decided to stop in the saloon first to get a beer and then to leave a message that Mason, Lane and those left of his gang would understand. We made it clear as glass what would happen to any of them. Particularly the message was aimed at Mason and Lane.

After a quiet night at the hotel, we all gathered outside the café. We were all ready to move on with the rest of our journey.

After a quick stop at the mercantile, we were ready to leave. Pa was the only one who knew the way. Tom said he was afraid he would get himself lost if he tried to find the mine. Pa had the map inside his head. He would not get lost. He guessed it would take at least a week to find the gold. Once that was done, we would then head east for Indian Territory to the Parks's place.

For me, this trip should be much easier for me than my trip west. Helen just stepped in and took over the cooking. She was the one who demanded that my bandages had to be changed.

With a few nights of good sleep and someone else's good cooking, I was ready to face whatever hurdles life would throw at us.

As we started out, we all knew that our problems had not gone away. Pa knew that we had to get to his hiding place without being found by Mason and his gang. Then we had to pack up the gold. Then we had to get to a big enough town that a bank could deal with the amount that Tom and Pa had mined.

Rufus came up with his first big idea. "Let's head for Anton Chico. It just lays some north and west. From there we can ride along the Pecos River."

We all thought that it sounded good, so we let Rufus take the lead. After a day of riding, we found ourselves in a quiet little town, right after sundown.

"I knows an hombre who lives here. Old Manuel lives here with his wife and a passel of children. If they are still here, we will have a place to stay and food to eat for a day or two. It will give us a chance to get rested up, then we can head on to John's hidey-hole."

With that said, we stopped in front of a large adobe home. Rufus knocked on the door and yelled for Manuel to come to the door.

"Hola, Manuel."

The door was opened slowly, and a very large gun was poked through the opening.

"Gringo, you have caused my little ones to be woke up. For this, I should shoot you, but I am trying to be a good man, so leave now and I will not shoot you. But do not anger me again with your rude behavior."

Rufus just stood there grinning real big and said again, "Let us in, amigo. I got friends who need some tending to." It was then that Manuel recognized that it was Rufus, and he opened the door wide.

"Hola, Senor Rufus. Now I see it is you! It must be a serious problem that brings you to my door so late in the evening. Come in. Come in."

"You got that right, my friend. Can you feed us a meal or two and take care of our animals for a day or two? We got to keep it quiet like. Understand?"

"What I have is yours, amigo. You and your friends, please come in. Mamacita, quickly. Senor Rufus and his friends have need of food and a place to sleep. Senor Rufus, names of your friends, please. Por favor."

"Oh, yes. This is Senor John, Senor Tom, and Senor John's daughter, Helen. These two are his sons, Matt and Jamie."

"Pablo, get your lazy self up and help these two young men to take care of their horses and mules. Rapido!" he said with a kick to the boy's hind end.

With that, Jamie and I went back outside to help with the animals and the wagon. Pablo showed us where to store the saddles, horses, Rufus's mule, and Clyde, along with the wagon. Between the three of us, we were done in no time. Manuel had a strong barn and corral behind his home. As lamps were lit, we could see just how big his home really was. Pablo never said a word, just pointed to where things could be left and out of the weather. By the time we went back inside, the kitchen was full of women cooking and talking at a mile a minute. But the smells were so good that I knew just how hungry I really was. So was Jamie.

"Matt, this food smells like heaven. I'm so hungry I could eat a horse, hooves and all. Know what I mean?"

"Yes, brother. I'm there with you."

Rufus showed us where we could wash up, and then we all grabbed a plate and a fork and started into the food. What there was, there was plenty of it. We all had our fill of beans and tortillas and several fried eggs over the top.

Apparently, Manuel had the best hen layers within a hundred miles. Two of Manuel's boys spent most of the time each day watching for hawks, coyotes, and two-legged robbers who tried to take off with the hens and their eggs. The boys sure were good at their job. One of the things I had to stay away from were those red chili peppers. Those peppers could set you on fire with just one bite. Watching Manuel and the children, it seemed the peppers were candy. It took several cups of water to stop the burning after just a small bite.

"Better look and see if that burn went all the way through the soles of your boots, young man." Manuel laughed with everyone else.

It wasn't long after the meal that we all headed to the hayloft to get some well-needed sleep. Helen was done worn out after all she had been through. My hope was that the time going back to Indian Territory would help her body and soul to heal. Maybe the rest of us could use some of that healing ourselves. For her, hopefully, the long road was going to lead to a more tranquil life for sure. It felt so good to have this many of the family together again, not counting Ardith. Then I thought of Audrey. I took a big breath, closed my eyes, and focused on to fall a peaceful night's sleep.

It was the next morning when our plans met with one more difficulty.

To me it was like this. "One more time!" As if there had been enough time to say anything to anyone at all.

Pa and I had started for the stable to get the rigs on the horses and hitch up the wagon. Pa was looking out over my shoulder when he whispered to me, "We got trouble, son. Be ready."

I heard the footsteps of several men. It sounded like three or four men at least were standing right behind me. I took a chance and bent down to pick something up with my left hand when the spokesman of the group said his piece.

"Lookee here now. See what we done found! We got us the boy who's been killing so many of our friends and his pa too. How do, John. We missed you back at the camp. Maybe we still get a chance to get some gold, boys. Yes, sirree!"

With his left hand in front his chest, Pa extended three fingers. He was letting me know that there were three men behind me. I looked up to Pa and said real loud so they could hear me while I still had my back to them. "Think they planning to give us an even break, Pa?"

"Not these three. They wouldn't give their own mother a break. Right, boys?"

"You said that right, Allison. You and the boy just drop your guns and ease up on your feet, and we'll just head right back to our old camp. Lane will be so glad to see you again."

"I guess they mean business, Pa. We better do like they say. We don't want any trouble. Do we?"

With that said, I began to stand. They had not noticed that with the first step they had made, I had drawn my holstered gun and was already cocked as my left hand was drawing the belt gun and cocked it. Without a thought, I turned to face them and just started shooting. The first bullet was on its way when I fell to the ground and then fired both guns as one. Three men. Three bullets. They were three dead men.

I was already standing up when I saw Pa. He was just standing there with his gun in his hand.

"I never even got my gun out let alone fire it. You got all of them in just a few seconds."

With that, I turned and walked away without saying anything to Pa or Tom. Jamie and the rest came running into the corral while I was reloading both guns. Two left, one right.

Tom was the first to speak and it was to me. "Matt, leave anything for the rest of us?"

"No, they just weren't up to the challenge. They should have been shooting more instead of talking. They just talked themselves into a grave."

As I walked away, I heard Pa questioning Tom.

"How in God's name did he do that? Those were some of the worst of Mason's gang. They shoot people at the drop of a hat. I didn't even get my gun into play before Matt had killed all three of them."

"Well, John. Matt there is probably one of the fastest gun hands in the west. I thought I was good, but Matt there is even better. A lot better. If the bad guys know it's him they must face, they know there is no letup with him. He is on the prod all the time. They know to look for a hole to jump in and stay away from him. Only thing they will get from him are bullets. And that is no lie."

Just to take some of the attention from me, I told Pa, "Go and check their guns, Pa. I think you will see that I had an edge. Tom taught me to listen for things that are not always thought of by most. Just look. You will see what I mean."

With that, Pa bent over and picked up the first gun. He saw immediately what I already knew without looking. It was not cocked. Nor were the other two. It was one more time when one of Tom's lessons had saved us. Tom always harped on this one important fact. If you were going into a shooting match, make sure the weapon was ready to fire. Never leave anything until the last minute or seconds. That's when seconds count. Being real sudden usually catches most people not being prepared. It surely did this time. They just talked too much.

"These three got just what they deserved. They were some of those who were at the cabin. There will not be any tears for the like of them. Not from me!"

Pa just looked at me for a moment and bent and helped Tom with hauling the dead ones off to the side. Manuel was agreeable to bury them. No dead bodies would leave nothing for Mason and Lane any reason to bring trouble for Manuel and his family.

We were ready to get on down the road, and Trinidad seemed the next place to stop. Going that direction might throw Mason and the gang off. Deep down inside, I was hoping that the killings would stop and soon. It was hard for me to keep the killings out of my mind. They all seemed to run into each other. I was just hoping I would not have to kill anymore.

At least for a day or two.

Chapter 26

As we traveled west, Pa reminded us about Mason and his gang.

"These men will never stop. They just don't know how. We must all stay sharp and be prepared. Don't let up, ever. Let's all think about the end of the road."

Pa was calculating how far we had to go, how to get the raw gold into a bank, then back to Indian Territory.

Pa decided partway to Trinidad that we were going down south, back to Taos. Helen was trying to hang in there with all the riding, even though she was riding on the wagon. She had been through too much. That was what decided Pa on the change of plans. As we rode down main street, we all decided that the La Fonda Hotel was the place to stay. We could take a few days to recuperate and get some strength back. Jamie and I took the reins of the animals and walked them to the stables while the rest of the group got rooms for us all. It only took a few minutes before we joined the rest back at the hotel.

The La Fonda was situated on the south side of the plaza. Late afternoons were cool under the veranda on the front of the hotel. Those not cleaning up were sitting and taking in the quiet time. After taking turns using the tubs out back, we all looked cleaner. For me, I was so glad to be clean. I had smelled so bad I couldn't stand my own smell. Sweat and gunpowder stayed on me for too long a time. For me, I was glad to ease up some. I still couldn't stop worrying about gunfights and being constantly alert. It was all pulling on me. The most recent bullet wounds I had were still tender to the touch, but they were healed good enough. It was the ones of the spirit that would take a little longer.

While I was feeling the warm water in the barrel, I realized that I had to have some new clothes. The clothes that I had taken off were so ragged that they needed to be thrown away. Pa had just dressed and was just leaving when I asked him if he could go to the mercantile and get me some clothes from the skin out.

Pa's only reply was, "It sure is time. Those rags were about to leave you naked as a jaybird. So yes, I will get you some appropriate clothing."

Pa was back in ten minutes with a pile of clothes that fit just fine. The water in the tub was getting cold, so I was more than glad to dry off and get those clean clothes on. Pa's choices were more elegant than I would have chosen, but he had in mind that we were staying in an elegant hotel and eating there required some manners along with the clothes.

As I walked through the hotel to join the rest of the family on the veranda, I saw a stranger who had just joined them. The stranger had just got started with some tale when Pa saw me. He asked the stranger to join us. The group were at the table enjoying some real home-cooked food. Taking Pa's invite to heart, the stranger joined us in the restaurant. While we were eating, the stranger was always talking about anything and everything.

While they were all talking, I just sat back out of the conversation and looked over this friend of Pa's. From head to foot, he was the typical westerner. His pants and shirt were faded by too much sun, wind, and rain while his boots were of the style preferred by men who spent most of their time in the saddle. The heels of his boots were narrowed down and angled to fit his stirrups. Dangling from his heels were large roweled Mexican spurs that made music as he walked across the floor. The gun he wore at his hip seemed a natural part of his body. He would have looked strange without it. I knew how it felt without my revolvers on. I felt naked and with nothing to use to protect myself or those I loved. The stranger's voice was all Irish brogue, which was hard to follow as he spoke to us.

"Just slow yourself down, Zeb. Here, meet my boys, Matthew and Jamie. Boys, this here is Zeb Harrison. He's another one of the group of trappers that helped us out when we were out here looking for gold. The truth of the matter is that they helped us out when we were being attacked by some Apaches, and then we helped them later with a gang looking to take their furs and some gold nuggets. It's too long a story to get into. Just know that they are our friends. They are men who you can trust no matter what!"

With a pause, he asked for the facts from Zeb. He had made himself a part of our little band and kept it to himself until now.

"Well, as I was trying to say. I had been hiding back off the trail for a day or more after seeing you, the boys, and Rufus. It wasn't long before I seen Cherokee Lane and about eight of Mason's gang heading for town with their rifles out and primed for bear. Iffen you folks want to stay and deal with this passel of varmints, I can holler up a friend or two and we can kill at least one or two before they start running back into the hills. Yes, sirree!"

Zeb seemed to sound like he was sorry he had missed all the shooting that had already happened. Hearing the name of Cherokee Lane caused a pause. We knew who Lane was, have known him since Missouri. But to play along, I asked the normal question.

"Who's Cherokee Lane?"

"Well, son, he is one of those who you do not want to have to face in a gunfight. Not now nor ever. He's as deadly as a rattler and twice as quick."

Having just said those words, Pa took a closer look at me with a strange look in his eyes.

"Why are you looking at me like that, Pa?"

"I'm just wondering how fast you are, Matt. I think if anybody could face Lane, it would be you. Not that I want you to make that attempt. Not at the chance that you could be hurt or killed. You surely showed me just how fast you were at Manuel's corral. That fight still makes me shake my head at how fast you were."

"Mayhaps you are right about the boy. I's hear tell that the boy is as fast as the best of them. Some folks are calling him Matt Guns.

Most folks did not know his last name, so they just used what seemed best to call him—Matt Guns. That's nothing to laugh at, not at all!"

It seemed the best time for Tom to tell the whole story. Pa needed to hear the rest of the story of our trip from Tennessee to Indian Territory and now here in New Mexico territory. In the past, I tried to say as little as possible about our trip, but Pa wanted to know it all, so that's why Tom did the talking, knowing that I was not one to brag or bring attention to myself. I just sat back and let him do the talking.

When the telling was done, Pa took a long look at me and said just a few words.

"That's been a lot of killing, son. Let's hope very soon the killing will end. I know you will always do your best and stand on the right side of the law. I certainly can't begin to understand what you and your younger brother have gone through. My part has been nothing in comparison. Just know I'm here for you all!"

With that, he squeezed my shoulder and walked away.

Pa never asked again about any of the shootings, whether they were necessary or not. I think that he knew that killing just one person was a load to carry. Killing so many was a greater weight. Every night I always asked the good Lord to help me with dealing with all that had happened for the last year and a half. It was only with his help could I ever make my way through it all.

Zeb talked right up. "Well, I must be going, John. I just wanted that you should know what news I had. Lest I forget, Lane and his gang are only a day's ride behind me. You best keep your guns handy. They'll be here sooner than you might think. Adios!"

"See you later, Zeb. Take care of yourself. Thanks for the news. Keep your scalp on" was all Pa had to say.

Zeb strode as lively as a spring colt across the room and out to his horse. It never ceased to amaze me the number and caliber of friends which my father and Tom had made since being out west.

We spent the remainder of the evening talking of the things we had not talked of since he had left us before the war. Some things were hard to talk about, but we worked through them just the same.

It was later that evening when the conversation landed on the topic of the gold.

"Tom told us that the secret was in that fool Comanche rattle you sent home for Jamie when he was a baby." I was sitting at the table, and I had been rolling the rattle around during our talking. Jamie and I had decided that I would keep the rattle with me. We felt that we might need it at some time in the future. That future was now.

"Well, there really isn't any secret to it actually."

With that said, Pa pulled the rattle to him and held it in his hands. With a twist of the handle, he popped it out of the top where the bones or whatever was used to make the rattle noise were. Pa lifted it so that the bones, which were really deer teeth, fell out on the table. He then used his pinkie finger to ease out a roll of parchment from inside the rattle. Then he put the bones back in and then fastened the handle back in place and gave it back to me.

What Pa rolled out was a map of where the mine was located. He used his finger to trace out the route to the mine and then from there to where they had left the gold dust and nuggets. That was the gold that they had planned to use in bringing the family out west and establish a ranch for cattle and horses. Pa had a way of describing the plans and desires that he and Tom had so worked hard for.

"Know this. Even if Mason had found the rattle and found the map, it would not have helped him in finding anything. There's a code that goes with the map that locates the gold."

It was then that I could see the numbers and letters around the edge of the map.

"What do they mean, Pa?"

"Just look at them for a minute or two, boys, and then think back on what you were taught. It was all done with both of you in mind!"

I sat there with the map in front of me, and I started looking around the edges. I turned it around just one time, and then Jamie put his hand on the map, and we both said together, "I see the meaning of what you have done."

"Pa, that was some pretty smart thinking on your part. Only Jamie and I could have known the code. Does Tom know the code?"

"No. Not even Tom knew the code. He was there with me, and he knew where the mine was located, but he did not know where I had stashed the bigger portion of the gold. That was after Tom left to lead Mason and his cronies away.

I thought back of how Pa had started when we were just old enough to read words, and he started teaching us the code. It was simple but only if a person knew the key number and letters to decode the message. Without the key, no one would know what was said on the map or any message Pa might have sent to us or us to him. I knew that in just a few minutes I could unravel the code and know what message he had left for us, including dates, times, and distance. Knowing all that, I handed the map back to Pa and sat back with Jamie, waiting for what more he might need to say.

After just a few minutes with nothing more to say, Pa rolled up the map and replaced it into the rattle and handled it back to me.

"You just hang on to the map and the rattle, son. There may come a time when you or Jamie need to return back to where the gold is hidden. It's like having an ace in the hole before having to play out your hand here."

"Okay, Pa. We'll all go together and get the gold. Once that's done, we can all head back to Indian Territory. You'll like Brand's ranch. That is who the Parks work for. It does remind me some of Tennessee, but it also has a better feel to it. Maybe it's something about the cattle, horses, chickens, and such. But I think it is the open spaces. You'll know what I mean when we get there, Pa!"

"Sounds like your anxious to get back there. Could it be that there's more than one reason to hurry along? From what Tom was saying earlier, I'm going to guess that it must be a girl. She must be a wonderful young lady to get you in such a state. You have truly grown up on me, Matthew."

My only acknowledgement of the truth was to blush and rub my toe on the leg of the table. Pa reached across the table and rumpled my hair with his work-hardened hand, and then he pulled me to his chest and gave me a hug that he had never done before, not that I ever remembered.

"Boy, it's going to be hard for all of us. I miss your ma way down deep inside. I know that it hurts for you boys and the girls in the same way. I'm so sorry for all those times when I was gone for months on end. When I did get home, she'd have things all shipshape and as neat as a pin. She could always make do with whatever she had. The little bit of money I could send to her, she made do. Her smile and her love were beyond measure to me. All this gold that Tom and I found was to make things easier for her. Instead, it caused her death. Lordy, how I'm going to miss her."

"I know, Pa. Jamie and I felt the same way. We buried her and little Jenny out back of the cabin under that crab apple tree she loved so well. If you are wondering why I'm so quick on the shoot with Mason's men, it goes back to what they did to Ma, little Jenny, Jamie, and the girls. Don't ask me to change. The only word that would describe how I feel is revenge. I have promised Ma, as she was dying in my arms, that I would not stop until the last one of that gang that had anything to do with all that happened that day were going to die."

"Yes, son. I do understand. I would not think to ask you to change or feel any different. Just know this, do not let this dark emotion totally consume you. Take some time to grieve and let go of the pain. Mason, Lane, and the rest will get what they have coming. Perhaps it will come from someone else. Just don't let it all make you into someone just like them. Understand, son, I love you and always will. Know that you will always have a home, a place you can hang up your hat and gun and feel at peace. Just keep that all in mind. Let's all get some sleep. We'll be up before sunlight. It will be a hard day, so savor the sleep you get. Tomorrow will be another day. Good night!"

"Good night, Pa!" was all that Jamie and I spoke together.

Chapter 27

The next morning, Helen had breakfast ready when Pa, Tom, and Rufus sat with the rest of us. They had the horses saddled and the wagon hitched. My mind was still looking toward the east when Pa said it was time to hit the trail. We were all anxious to get started. With that, I turned my mind to what was at hand. Time to find the gold!

The area we were traveling through was an area that a Spanish gent, Alvarodo, had passed through in 1540, on a journey from Taos to Pueblo. Pa had been telling us some of the local history, and he emphasized what he wanted us to remember. He and Tom had picked up some of the history themselves from their last trip this way. We listened and filed away the information. We could think on it another time and a later place.

We had only been gone from the town by just a few hours when we could see the dust of a group of horsemen heading into the town from the south. By the time that group could get there and then find out that we were not there, they would be at least half a day or more behind us. That was just fine with me. If they tried to come upon us, we would know it. We would know where they were and how long before they could get close to us. We were each taking turns hanging back to watch our back trail. No one would catch us napping. Not us. Not this time. Not ever.

We all knew that Mason and his gang were bound and deter-mined to ruin any of our happiness. They wanted the gold and our lives. The only way for us to feel at peace would be when that gang and their leaders were dead and gone.

There was one main idea that kept running through my brain. Before things were done, Cherokee Lane and I would have to face one another. I didn't care who was faster. I just planned on being the one still alive.

Rufus said that Lane could not keep from bragging what he was going to do to me if he had the chance. For the present, we would just rejoice in having Helen and Pa back with the family. Mason and Lane would just have to wait until we absolutely had to face them. Not before.

Me, I kept believing that this was a wonderful place to live, and the West would be a so much better place without the Masons and Lanes and their types of people around. Perhaps Pa was right. The legal law would eventually take over. It was happening in many places, but it was slow. But until then, people like us had to watch for and take care of these kinds of people. Sometimes with a bullet, sometimes with a rope. Many times, just life had a way of dealing with the worst kind.

The next morning dawned without any sign of Mason's gang. We knew that it was only going to be a short reprieve. They would never give up searching for the gold or those who possessed it. Since that was us, we had to stay on our toes and not let them get close to us. If they were to find us, they would kill us all and we would be gone from the face of the earth. Our job was to turn the tables on them.

Zack Mason was not one to give up on anything that he wanted as bad as he wanted that gold. He wanted it and wanted it badly. The men he had lost meant nothing to him. He could always get more of the same caliber. For him, it was the gold. He was so mad for it, it had cost him the one person who he had ever loved. Ma! Now I knew what drove him. Pa had finally told us the rest of the story. Ma had spurned Mason and went with Pa. Mason could never forgive or forget that. For that reason, he hated Pa with a passion.

It was noon, so we stopped for a rest. Pa started talking about the situation.

"The thing we must get straightened out is what we must do when things start happening. One, we could keep going on and get the gold and head for Denver. Or two, we could head back to Indian Territory and give it some time to settle down out here and then sneak back out and get the gold and get it into a bank without them knowing."

"Seems to me, Pa, that since we're this close to the gold, let's get it and make a run for Denver. Too many things could happen if we wait. With you to guide us, we can find it faster. After Denver, we can head back east to Indian Territory and then to wherever we plan to settle. Maybe we can do it and be done before Mason and his gang ever find us."

Tom was agreeing with me on this.

"Matt's right, John. Let's go and get the gold and then hightail it for anywhere there is a solid bank and some law to help deal with Mason and his gang. Besides, I'm some lonesome to get back to see the family back in Indian Territory myself."

Jamie was quick to speak up.

"Yeh, I'm sure Tom wants to get back to see Ardith. He sure got all puppy eyes when he was around her. You will have to keep an eye on him, Pa," he said with a smirk.

Pa turned to Helen and posed the question. "Helen, what do you think? You've been through more than any of us. You ready to head back to safer climes?"

"Yes, I am more than ready. But I'm just like Matt and Tom about the gold. Let's get it now and then get back to somewhere we can call home. To me, it makes more sense to get it now and deal with whatever happens later."

Not that it was needed, but Jamie and Rufus both agreed with the rest. The rest of that day, we stayed on the trail. We were all quiet considering all the things that might cause us any difficulties.

That night we had come to several conclusions. We were all in agreement on how to deal with Mason, Lane, and their gang. Rufus and I agreed to be the ones to hand back and do what could be done to hide our tracks. Hopefully we could send Mason and his gang in a different direction.

The next night was the first step in our ways of leading Mason and the rest in a wrong turn. Rufus and I took the two extra horses and used them to make a clear trail that headed north and then east.

Before leaving this last camp, Rufus and I spent an hour trying to cover up the trail left by the others. We left our horses hidden and walked for more than a mile brushing out what there was of their trail. Rufus and I felt that all was done that could be done.

Hopefully, Mason would think that we had decided to give up and had headed for Indian Territory or somewhere back east. We made a clear trail heading north for a half day's ride before we headed east. Rufus knew the area well, and he used the terrain to cover our trail unless they were right behind us. After another day's ride, we turned back west.

With Rufus's help, our own trail just disappeared. To do this, we rode for several miles in the narrow, shallow creek that would hide our prints. Then he led us out of the creek at a place the rock and sand would cover our tracks. Without an Indian scout who could read what was not there, we just disappeared, totally.

With that done, we made our way to the place where we had agreed to meet with the rest. They were right where they needed to be. They were in a little valley that only an Indian from the area would have found them.

Pa and the group were glad to see us and were ready to get moving down the trail. The next morning, we left the valley and found the trail Pa was looking for. He pointed some to the north and some west toward Wolf Creek Pass. Pa said that more snow fell there than any place he had ever seen in his life. Even in the middle of the summer, there were drifts of snow around the pass that could be six, eight feet deep.

Getting through the pass, we turned south to locate our last landmark, Turkey Creek.

Taking a break, Pa then told us what had happened years before. He said that it was pure luck that he and Tom had found any gold. How they found it was the work of someone else.

Back then, they had gotten as far as Fort Bent. There they met an old trapper who decided to give them the location of his claim.

He was heading back east and did not plan on ever returning. While talking, he drew them out a map with some further verbal direction. He believed there was enough gold in the mine for two young enterprising young men like us. He said that if we were willing to work hard, we could do very well. He said that the only problem that he knew of was the Injuns in the area. The Utes were causing all kinds of commotion and that we would have to be on our guard every minute of every day. We were to keep our rifles handy and our powder dry, was the way he put it to us.

He said, "Iffen you get the chance, look up the chief and you maybe can make a deal with him and the braves! Just think about that!"

Pa told us how they managed to get twisted around more than once before they found the right creek. Once there, they found the old trapper's diggings. He had given them a quick deed for the mine. So with the deed, it was legal if anyone came along and argued about their rights. They also had their guns for those who wanted to argue.

With the fear of Indians always lurking in their minds, they took turns at using the pick and shovel. It was a good way to share the load, so to speak. One worked and the other guarded. In no time at all, they had several bags of dust and a few small bags of nuggets. The old trapper had told them the truth. The gold was there and easy to get.

They both knew that winter was coming soon. They both had to stop their work on the mine and build a better shelter out of the old trapper's lean-to, so they could spend the winter. Every day one of them spent a few hours hunting for meat and gathering nuts or berries that were left over from the bears and such. They knew that winter would be a trial for them. There was no way out until spring when the snow would begin to melt. They used the final days left to cure the meat of several deer and an elk and one lonesome buffalo that must have been lost. They hoped that they would have enough food stuff that would last them through till spring. The hides of the animals would come handy during the coldest and snowiest winter they ever experienced.

Tom became the hunter because he knew how to make a bow and arrows. He could bring in meat without firing his rifle. The sound of a rifle could alert any Indians in the area that there were white men in the area. It could also be the cause of snowslides during the deep part of the winter.

Late in that first summer, their loneliness and silence was broken when Captain Pfeiffer, a close friend of Kit Carson's, dropped in on them. He was leading a scouting mission through that area. He was already a close friend of the Utes, and they valued his opinion. It was he also that recommended that they go and see the local chief and discuss their mining plans. Captain Pfeiffer never asked about the mine itself and stayed focused on his mission at hand.

Pa and Tom used the next two days to find the chief, who they found to be a far-thinking man. It was Chief Raven Wing himself who thought that the Utes could benefit from the mine as well as Tom and Pa. The chief talked with the other leaders of the tribe, and they agreed and granted them permission to continue to mine as long they would share the profits with the tribe. When Pa and Tom brought the first share of the ore, the chief made them both blood brothers to the tribe. They were highly respected for their honesty and bravery.

Chief Raven Wing knew from bitter experience that not all white men could be trusted. He had met our common enemy, Zach Mason and his gang, a few weeks before. Mason had lied to the chief with a lot of fast talk and then tried to murder him. Had Chief Raven Wing not been alert to the danger he was in, Mason would have succeeded. As it was, Chief Raven Wing was barely able to return to his camp, even though wounded. While the chief had turned his back to Mason, Mason had stabbed him and left him for dead. A pair of young braves had found him and helped get him back to their camp. His warriors had combed the area for Mason, but he seemed to have vanished. Too bad for us.

The rest of the story we knew too well—how the war and then being in the prison played out.

I just could not keep the thought out of my mind that Mason and Lane were out there somewhere and that they knew where we were. Our problem was just what he and his gang might have in store for us and what could we do to change things to our favor.

One thing that we all agreed on was that Mason and Lane and those left of his gang were not going to give up on the gold. What we had to do was do something that they would not consider.

If they thought we would find what was hidden and make a run for Denver, they were mistaken. Maybe a cold winter would push them off to somewhere where it would be warmer. Our plan was just the opposite. We planned to spend the winter right there.

We had brought more than enough supplies as we could use to hopefully see us through the winter. Our intention was to wait things out through the winter. We would work the mine as long the weather would allow, and then hunker down until early spring. As soon as the snow started melting and we could make it out, we would. In that way, we might be able to beat Mason and his gang to Denver City. Once the gold was in a bank, we could then head for Indian Territory.

We worked from sunup to sundown for several weeks and then winter came. It came with a vengeance. The wind moaned through the pines, and the snow piled up higher than my head. We had never seen the like in all our lives.

We were glad to be with Pa, Tom, and Rufus. These men knew how to survive this winter weather. Helen hated the weather and let us all know it. But she did the cooking and whatever without complaining. Thankfully, we all survived.

One day, clear out of the blue, I heard Jamie speaking to the sky and to anyone else who would bother to listen.

"Does it snow like this every winter? Seems to me that if it keeps on, we could load up a couple of sleds and we could make it to the prairie with just a little push. That would be one wild ride."

I turned to Tom and voiced my thought without thinking. "You reckon the folks back at the Indian Territory have forgotten us?"

"No. They knew how long it might take us to get this job done right. The Parks are good folk. They'll not be forgetting us anytime soon. What with spring we'll be seeing them again. Don't you worry none. I know that Audrey for sure will be there waiting for you. Don't let that negative thought linger in your head. Think on other things."

Christmas and then New Year's 1870 came and went without any great notice from us there in the vast wilderness. Jamie was keeping track of the date on a tree stump with knife marks. I was twenty, and Jamie was sixteen. We had promised ourselves that we would have our own celebrations when we got back to the Territory.

Finally, it came to the last days of March, and the snow drifts were beginning to melt away. Then we were into April before we started to see the green tops of grass. The days continued to get warmer, and we knew it was time to leave.

For Helen, Jamie, and me, this winter had been a learning experience. Pa, Tom, and Rufus tried to teach us all they could on how to live through the worst of weather conditions.

The biggest lesson was the easiest one. Never get in a big hurry in extreme cold, winter weather. Take your time and roll with the punches it gave.

As hard as this country could be, Jamie and I along with Helen had really come to love it. Maybe not so deep in the mountains, but the foothills were the place. Waking up in the morning and seeing the mountains to the west and the long plains that lay to the east were glorious. Pa and Tom both talked that this was some of the best land to raise cattle and horses.

Me, I had been thinking that same thought from the very first time we got into the foothills. Someday this would be the place for Audrey and me. I knew that I was hoping. Who could tell. Time would tell.

One day, I was reminded of those thoughts when Jamie was thinking out loud to himself. "We got to come back here. All this beauty is just too much to take in after only this short time we have been here. Don't ya think, Matt?"

"Yes, I do! I know what you're saying. Maybe after this situation is done we can bring the whole family out here and settle in a permanent place!"

"I agree, Matt. We all need a change. I want a place to just sit and drink it all in. That will give us all time to heal and complete the grieving process." That was Pa speaking his mind without any encouragement from either of us.

Chapter 28

Spring came with a rush of wind and easy showers that brought out the elk, deer, along with bears, panthers, and hunters. Chief Raven Wing's tribe were our friends, but there were others around who were our enemies, so we stayed alert. We knew that Mason's gang could be waiting for us. Knowing that, it was time to head on out.

Pa made the decision. It was time to leave. With that said, we started packing what we would need. The extra horses and the mules would be needed to haul the gold to wherever we were going. Denver City was talked as the most likely place to go. We kept one horse for our grub, and we carried all we could in the wagon. The two mules would have a pull, but if necessary, the extra horses could help pull. In a day, we were ready to go.

This past winter had been good for Pa. I could see that the memory of Ma was still there for him, but he had moved past the grief.

Tom mentioned more than once to Jamie and me, "Your pa is a one-woman kind of man. Don't know if another woman could take your mothers place!"

In my mind, no woman would ever be able to take Ma's place. Well, time would tell. To me, I felt that Pa was still too young a man to live alone the rest of his days. But it would be up to him how he would live his life.

The one thing we all had to consider was Zach Mason and Cherokee Lane and their gang. Whichever place we headed for, we had to keep them in our minds and our plans. For me, the sooner than later was how I wanted it. Kill or be killed—that was what waited for us. As we knew too well, that Mason always had some trick up his sleeve.

"Let's get some things squared away before we get too far along on this here journey," Pa said as we paused on the trail to give the horses a blow. "This gold can still cause many difficulties. If anything happens to me, you boys are to see that the girls get their share of the gold. Same as you boys get. I know that I can trust you boys to be fair with all that must be done."

Tom spoke up, "The same goes for mine too. Rufus is to get a share of mine, and the rest is to go to Ardith. You boys know how I feel about your sister. You just take good care of her for me if anything were to happen to me!"

Hearing them talk this way made me want to talk back to them about talking so negatively. But then I knew why. Jamie and I were in the same place. Only the good Lord would know how this whole thing would turn out. We only knew that we have this day here, and tomorrow will come with whatever troubles it can hold. If anyone could have heard me talking to myself, they would have thought I was turning into a preacher or a philosopher.

The days rolled by like the tumbleweeds that dotted the prairie. We had made a quick stop to pick up the other cache Pa had left hidden. That done, we headed north to Denver. We had no idea whatever fate awaited us. There were days when the skies would just open and soak us to the skin. It was always a mystery to me where all the rain came from.

"I can sure sympathize with them folks who suffered with the flood in the Bible. I can't begin to figger forty days and nights of rain. That would surely be a bit too much."

"That's right, Jamie. That's why God's plan was to fix this old world some better. That's why he allowed Noah to repopulate the earth. If only God could have left out the Zach Masons and Cherokee Lanes out of this world be so much better."

"It would have made it a better place, that's for sure" was my only reply.

We were only a few days away from Denver City. No one felt safe until we got the gold into a bank. We were all riding with our rifles on our saddle bows and our pistols were lose and ready for any kind of fight that could happen.

We made our way to Denver City without any problems. Obviously, the Indians had been other places, causing problems for other folks. We never saw a nary one.

"Listen up. We must stay on our toes. It's a big town but still has enough outlaws too. Let's be ready for any problems that might occur in a town like Denver" was Pa's admonishment.

We all rode guard around the wagon until we got to the bank. While Pa and Tom took care of the bank business, Helen, Rufus, Jamie, and I decided to see the town.

It was agreed that we would never leave Helen alone anywhere in town. For that reason, we all hung out together. We all knew that Mason was evil enough to try to abduct Helen again and use her against us. But it never happened because we never let anyone close enough to touch her let alone try to kidnap her.

The bank clerk had drawn up letters of credit for each of us to use on large purchases. The bank clerk had taken the time to remind each of us that the letters were just like money in the pocket. Lose them or have them stolen would be on our heads, not the banks. His last words were for us all. "Put them in a place where no one could find them and never show them to anyone unless used to be pay for purchases you need." We all knew what he meant.

After a few days in Denver, it was time to head for Indian Territory. We loaded the horses and the mules on an empty cart on the train headed east. We all got to ride the train to Newton, Kansas.

After a few days in Newton, we saddled the horses and headed south and east for the Indian Territories. We got south to Wichita, Kansas, and Pa said we could stop for at least a day or two at the trading post. He said it was the one that James Mead had set up many years before. Pa always loved to tell us those little nuggets of history on people, places, and things that had happened. He said that Meade and Jesse Chisholm had decided to set up a place to handle trade with Indians and the myriad of settlers that would be coming west to find their place on the frontier. It was there we planned to head southeast into Indian Territory and toward the ranch on the Verdigris River.

It started as a hot, dry, and dusty June day. Nothing had changed by the time we got to the trading post. Jamie and I were eager to take care of the horses while the rest went to the big log cabin that served as the store, eatery, and post office. There was nothing but a pole corral for the horses and a small shed for our gear to keep it out of the rain.

Our plan was to spend a day here and then move on. Jamie and I took a few minutes to look over the horses and Clyde. We had kept Clyde for carrying our camping gear and such. We took enough time to check their hooves for any loose shoes, clean their hooves, and see that there were no back sores from the saddles or packs.

We had just finished with these chores and were heading for the front door.

"Let's go see what everyone else is up to, Jamie."

Halfway there, we both heard a noise coming from the trail. We stopped and looked to the south to identify what was coming. A large cloud of dust was coming our way. In just a few seconds we could see that it was a group of riders heading our way.

"I don't like the looks of this bunch. We best get inside and tell them about this bunch coming in."

Jamie was only a step behind me as we sprinted for the store. It was then we noticed that there was another bunch of riders coming in from the north. We were boxed in. The showdown was finally here. It could be no other than Zach Mason and his lousy bunch.

"Pa, we got company. Two bunches, one from the north and another from the southwest. Looks like about ten or twelve all together."

"All right, Jamie. Let's see if we can catch them off guard."

Pa turned to Tom and Rufus, and with a few words, explained his brief plan to us all as he and the store owner passed out double-barreled shotguns to several of us, including Helen.

"Helen, you stay put here in the store and do whatever you can to help. But please stay out of harm's way."

"Don't worry about me. I'll do my part. There are some in this bunch who I would love to see over the sights of a shotgun."

It took only a few moments for Jamie, Rufus, and me to find our own hiding places. Pa and Tom waited only a few moments before the two gangs rode into the dusty street in front of the store. When the two groups finally came to a stop, that was when Pa and Tom stepped out to face them.

Pa took one more step to the edge of the veranda and looked Zach Mason in the eye. It was several minutes before Mason was forced to break off the eye contact with Pa.

Mason turned to Lane. "Don't draw yet. Let's see what John has to say!" As the staring contest started back up, Tom slid off to one side of Pa. He was one long step from the water barrel that sat there, which was a good place for him to fire from behind it.

Finally, Mason broke the silence again.

"We've come a long way to get to this point, John. You could have saved us all a lot grief if you had just given the gold to us the first time."

Pa just answered right back, "What right do you think that you have to that gold or any gold that you didn't earn rightly. Tom and I labored hard for many weeks for what we have. We worked up sweat, gave blood, and wore blisters to get what we did. Not you or any of this bunch of back shooters and lazy do-nothings have any right to any of it. You were always a greedy and selfish boy, and you still are. You are a worthless, piss-poor man. You never took any responsibility for anything that ever happened and were never satisfied at anything or anyone. Just like now!"

"I'm surprised that you think that I would be so stupid as to keep the gold with us. It is safe and sound in a bank back in Denver City. That's a place where you will never get your hands on any of it now, or ever. The best for you to do is to turn around and ride out of here. That's the only way that a great percentage of you and this bunch will get to live beyond the next few minutes."

"Well, well. There is just no fooling you, John. You're out numbered. Gold or no gold, you are the one who is going to be dead. However, Lane here feels that he has a score to settle with that son of yours. The one they're calling Guns. Now, I can see Tom, but where is Rufus and the others? There are several here who want to settle up with them. Where are they, John?"

"They've already gone on to Indian Territory. They took Helen back to be with her sister and friends."

Lane just couldn't wait to chime in with his two cents' worth.

"Where at is that boy of yours, John. I aim to shoot out his eyes before we hang you and that other whelp from a tree. Surely, he would not have ran away from a fight. Would he?"

That was my cue to step out from behind Lane and to his left. I had used the time while they were talking to get to where I was standing. I had checked my pistols and had added an extra bullet to both guns. Five bullets would not be enough, not even six. But for Lane, that should be enough. And they were cocked, and I was ready.

"Looking for me, Lane?" I said as I stepped out.

He had started to turn his mount when my talking had stopped him in his tracks.

"Get down from your horse, Lane. I don't want anyone to say that I took undue advantage of you when I kill you!"

Lane laid the reins on the neck of his horse. As he laid his hands on his weapons, his words to me were this. "Boy, you done chewed off more than you can swallow. Goodbye."

With that said, he dropped to the offside of his horse, pulling his guns as he landed. That was his loss. My guns were already banging away before he fired his first shot. His only shot went into the ground between my feet with no effect at all. Both of my shots though had taken Lane in the gut. That was all I could see under the belly of his horse. So that was where the shots went.

As his guns fell from his hands, he fell into the dirt. Lane seemed amazed for just a second. "Boy, you done went and killed me!"

My answer was loud enough for all of them to hear.

"Yes, you are dying. You were the one who killed Ma and little Jenny. You were the one who shoved Mason's gun from killing one of your fellow murderers. You have gotten exactly what you earned."

Lane rolled over, coughed once, and was dead. I saw a movement from the man next to Mason, who had his gun up to shoot, and so I shot him out of his saddle.

"Anyone else have the desire to die today?"

Tom then called out to two men who he could see in the group. "You two, step down and step away from the others. Try to draw, and I'll shoot you both without a thought."

Some of the gang were starting to get antsy.

Tom spoke to Pa, "These two are mine, John. Ardith was real clear about those who had misused her."

With that, Tom turned and got their attention. He dropped his gun into his holster and yelled, "Draw!"

Tom drew so fast that the two never had a chance. That made it four men dead in that many minutes.

"Well, Mason. That is four men dead. Would you like to try for two or three more? Perhaps you would like to take me on. No, I know you. You are too much of a coward and scared to try to do it yourself. Am I right, Zach?"

Then Tom spoke up for all to hear. "Don't be a damn fool, Zach. Give it up. Your pet snake is dead and three more besides. If you haven't noticed, we got you boxed in. Rufus is behind you to the left and Jamie is to the right. If I was a betting man, I would guess that Helen has a shotgun pointed at your smiling face. Give it up. Go away and never show up anywhere any of us may live or visit. We are tired of this crap now and forever! Understand?"

Mason took a minute to look around the yard and the front of the store, and he could see that Tom was right. Helen had a shotgun aimed at him and anyone else within ten feet of him.

Mason said to this gang. "Men, don't try anything."

Then Mason looked at Pa. "Don't be thinking this is over. Just remember, somewhere, sometime, I'll be there when you don't expect it to happen. There will be another time. Count on it."

With that said, Mason pulled his horse around with the remains of his gang and started to ride away.

That was when Rufus stepped out from his hiding place, right in front of Mason and his gang. There were at least one more thing to be done before they could leave. They all saw the shotgun he was carrying just like the one that Helen and Jamie were pointing at them.

"John, we should pull their fangs, don't you reckon? This bunch are too timid for my likes. You boys all reach with your left hands and undo those belts and drop your guns to the ground. All of them. Anyone who wants to dislike this call, just try to do something about it."

With that said, all of them dropped their gun belts.

"Let's drop those rifles along with any hideout guns, boys."

There were a few more weapons that ended in the street. Pa directed Jamie to pick up the weapons and throw them in our wagon. In just a few minutes, it was done.

Pa's last words to Mason were quick and to the point.

"We are leaving tomorrow morning. If we see any dust coming up behind us, we will set up an ambush and we will kill every last one of you. If there are any problems or if one of us gets hurt or dies accidental like, we will start hunting for every last one of you. We will kill you where we find you. Think carefully before you act against us again. You will get your weapons from Mr. Meade here three days from now. There will be no trouble in Wichita. The people who live here will keep their eyes and rifles on you as you ride back in. These people here know who you are and what you are capable of. They will shoot first and ask questions later. Do you understand? Yes, Mason, you and I will have another day soon. But know that it will be your last one on this earth. Leave me and mine alone, and you might live to be an old man. Start anything and you will die. Remember, no one will mourn for you!"

With that said, Mason and his gang rode away. They headed straight west. We all kept watching them until we couldn't see them. Only dust was still hanging in the air.

We had a quick conversation, and it was decided that we were leaving town as soon as possible. Doing that would put some miles between us and Mason's gang. We had been very lucky this time. It could have been a bloodbath. People here could have been hurt or killed along with anyone in our group. With that in mind, we gathered the things we needed and headed south to the Indian Territories.

It was decided that we could rest better when we got to the Parks's place.

We followed the east bank of the Arkansas River for the rest of the day to a likely camping site. As we sat around the campfire, I could feel the eyes of everyone staying on me longer than was necessary. It made me some uncomfortable. Finally, Pa was the one to speak up.

"Son, you were real sudden with those guns. You got to tell me how you knew when to draw against Lane. Everyone said he was one of the fastest. That was some shooting, son!"

Before I could speak up, Tom spoke for me.

"John, you didn't see what they did to Kathryn and little Jenny. Nor how bad young Jamie was shot up. They all got just what they deserved. Don't ride the boy. Lane has had it coming for years. This world has been downright rough for Matt and Jamie and the girls."

"John, I believe that Matt has a good sense of the right and wrongs of things. He knows better than most when to shoot and when to talk."

"It's all right, Tom. I can speak for myself."

I looked Pa straight in the eyes as I answered his spoken and unspoken questions.

"They declared war on us back in Tennessee. I told you before that was when I swore an oath on Ma and Jenny's grave. I had promised that I would do all I could to bring them all to judgement. On their side, they had sworn that they would shoot any of us on sight, so I figured that same intention was my own. No quarter asked for, none given. As far as Lane, his mistake was when he decided to jump from his horse. I had my guns out and cocked before he dropped from his horse. He had his gun out, but he had no chance to aim that first shot. By that time, I had already shot him twice. That was another one of the things I learned from Tom. He always said to shoot what you can see. Don't wait for nothing else!"

"Matt, you are only eighteen. Don't you think there has been enough killing?"

"Sorry to tell you, Pa, you lost track of time. I'm nineteen right now and will turn twenty come December this year, iffen it's 1870.

Age is not the issue. The thing is, we got to be prepared. If we let up, Zach Mason and his gang will be standing on the doorstep with guns in their hands. He aims to see us all dead. The man has a terrible hate for us."

Jamie chimed in, "Why is that, Pa? We should have killed him when we had the chance at Wichita. Why didn't we? You said yourself that he hated you because of Ma!"

"Boys, you are both real sudden with those guns. You both have killed quite a few men. I'm guessing that Lane was the deadliest of the lot. No one will miss him. The question is, How are you both doing emotionally? All this killing must leave a mark on a person. At another time, I will explain the rest of the Mason story."

"All right, Pa! I know there is a time and place for everything. But hear me now! Leave me be! I'll deal with the feelings left over because of the killings at another time. Now is just not the time. Me, I am just fine and dandy with the way things have gone so far."

With so much said, it was time for everyone to sleep. That was for everyone but me. I lay there thinking about what Pa had said. I never slept, and then it was my turn to guard. I was hoping that sleep would be better once I could see Audrey. It would be only a few more days and we would see them.

Truly, I was nineteen. Twenty was just around the corner. I just wasn't sure that I was ready to settle down. Pa was right. I do need some time and deal with these emotions after it is all done.

One thing I did know was that I loved Audrey. But it was not enough right now to get me settled down. Not just right yet.

Chapter 29

It was a week later when we arrived in Brand's ranch. I thought I knew hot weather, but this was nothing I could compare with. The wind and the heat were unbearable. The humidity was even worse. We literally soaked our clothes with sweat with very little effort. There was just no escaping it.

As we walked our horses into the clearing in front of the ranch house, we could see that much had changed while we were gone. The house that Eli had promised his missus was complete. It even had a fancy front porch and whitewash to boot. The barns and sheds showed that Eli and his crew had cared for them with an eye to the future and with some pride.

I sat my horse and quietly looked around while the rest of our group were dismounting. Somewhere I heard a door slam and the sound of running feet. With a rush, Ardith, along the whole Parks family ran to meet us. I found Audrey hanging at the back of the group. She and I saw each other, and I could see in her eyes that everything was good between us. Audrey seemed as though she had lost someone and now that person was found, and that someone was me.

I slipped off Duke, and Audrey was standing there waiting for me. Without a word, she was in my arms and squeezing me so hard that she almost broke a rib or two. For just a moment, the rest of the group and the whole world did not matter as she raised her face up to me. Never had she kissed me with such passion. It was such a feeling that it swept through me like a prairie fire.

"I always knew that you would come back. I just knew. Ardith did too. We both knew that everything would work out fine. We just had to keep our love strong for you and Tom."

Even as a part of me was reveling in the attention from Audrey and the others, there was a part of me that remained detached.

Something didn't feel right to me. What was it? Everyone was smiling and laughing, and I was standing there with Audrey, trying to smile, but only a frown showed. Rufus saw the look on my face and started to glance around the yard. I was doing the same. It was something I feared to hear, and Rufus was hearing the same thing. It was the sound of running horses, and they were coming right at us!

"Tom, Pa, get the ladies inside as quick as you can. It's got to be Mason and his bunch, and they ain't here to make a social call!"

With that said, I grabbed my rifle off Duke as Rufus grabbed for his. We had to make this the last fight. I yelled at Audrey to run into the house and gave her a slight push to head her that way. I quickly turned my head and mind to the gunfight fixing to start right in front of me.

"Jamie, get the mules and the horses into the barn as fast as you can. Then find a place to shoot from" was Pa yelling orders.

"Damn it all. We should have killed Mason when we had the chance, Pa." These are words which I didn't usually use.

"Mercy is poorly served on the likes of Zach Mason. Just you remember that, boy," Rufus said, not Pa or Tom.

There was no more time for talking or giving sermons on Mason or his gang. They came riding fast into the yard with their guns out and shooting without any attempt to aim, just firing into the crowd.

Tom and I split up and rushed to each end of the porch to draw their fire away from the main part of the house. I started using my rifle but dropped it and started with my handguns. With them, I was dropping one man after another. Tom was doing the same from his end of the porch.

I was searching for Mason and hoping to put an end to this slaughter. That was when someone got in a lucky shot. The shot hit me in the left leg, again, knocking me down. I was down, and then I was trying to get back up. That was when Audrey was right there with me shooting my rifle that I had lain down on the edge of the porch. That was when I laid my eyes on Zach Mason. He was aiming deliberately right at Audrey. He was pulling the trigger on his gun just as I shot into him. Audrey fell to the ground as I pulled myself and put shot after shot into Mason, yelling with every shot.

"Mason, you're a dead man." I yelled at every step for everyone to hear above the roar of the guns. Every step, I shot into Mason. If I had stopped shooting sooner, Mason would have hit the ground like a bag of potatoes. I finally stopped when I was out of bullets. When that happened, Mason hit the ground dead. No more evil threats from him.

I started looking around at what had happened. It was over in just a few minutes. Most of Mason's gang were dead. Only one or two were still hanging to life. It meant nothing to me. Casually, I started reloading my pistols. While doing that, I allowed my eyes to see if there were any of them left who might try to shoot back.

Then I remembered Audrey. I holstered my guns and bent to lift her into my arms with tears in my eyes. I turned to walk up the steps to get her into the front door when Mr. Parks and Mr. Brand and his cowboys showed up. Mr. Parks came to me and reached for Audrey.

"Just take it easy, Matt. Let me help you with her. She's going to be okay. She's alive and will stay that way once we get her into her bed. Her mother will do what needs to be done."

He looked at me and said, "But, Matt, I think you need to sit down yourself."

He yelled for Tom, "Tom, could you help me with Matt? We need to stop this bleeding before he bleeds out." That was when I just almost passed out.

Mrs. Parks had arrived and started to give orders to the cowboys and her husband.

"Eli, you get Audrey into her room, right now. Ardith and Helen, one of you get some water to boil and the other can make some strips of cloth for bandages. John, you and Jamie see what else needs to be done to any of the ones left alive in the yard."

Tom took me by the arm and helped me to sit down on the steps to the porch.

"Looks like you got another leaker, Matt. It is just above the last one that just healed up." Tom poked and prodded around and declared that it was only a flesh wound.

"Jamie, could you go to our mule and find the medicine box and bring that ointment that's been used many times on us all. It has worked good on minor wounds, and we all know how much yelling Matt likes to make when it's used."

In no time, Tom had my wound cleaned and bandaged. I pushed off the steps and staggered my way up to Audrey's bedroom. Her mother was working carefully on her wound. She turned and spoke to me even as she worked.

"Audrey is going to be fine, son. The wound is on her left side. I think nothing bad has been done. The problem is that the bullet is still in there, and that is an operation that I cannot do. We are going to need a doctor to take care of that."

I was leaning against the door jamb when a rough hand touched my arm. Turning, I saw that I was looking into Rufus's face.

"If you would let me, boy, I think that I can be of service to the young lady. Long before I went west, I was a fairly good doctor. From time to time, I have been called upon to remove a few bullets, sewed up a few knife wounds, and even took care of a lucky chap that got scalped," he said, touching his bald pate. "You know what I mean. I'll take a peek and see what we can do to help the young lady!"

Pa was standing there close to me. He saw my eyes roll up, and the light went out in my mind. Had Pa not been there, I would have hit the floor. He held me up, and with help from Tom, they took me to another room and laid me down.

It was early the next day when I woke up. I looked around and could see that someone had cleaned my leg again and put a new bandage on. Someone had removed my jeans and then left a clean pair of jeans and a clean shirt along with my boots and such.

In just a few minutes, I was up and dressed and was leaving the room for Audrey's. As I knocked on the door, Mrs. Parks opened it up for me. She knew the concern on my face was real, and she let me know very quickly how Audrey was.

"She is doing well. Rufus did a wonderful job. She is still sleeping right now. Dr. Sheffield got here this morning, and he said that she should awake later today or tomorrow at the latest. He also said that Rufus did a great job. He even offered him a job if he wants one!"

Mrs. Parks and I sat there and talked for a few minutes more before she suggested that I get on downstairs and, if I was lucky, one of the girls could make me some breakfast. Everyone else had eaten and were out doing what had to be done.

Just like they all said, Audrey woke on the third day. I was sitting there, keeping an eye on her, when her eyes slowly opened. She turned her face toward me, and she smiled the biggest smile I had ever seen. I started to stand to get her mother when she said, "Stay. Stay, please. I was so scared that I had lost you to Mason that I lost my head and took your rifle and started shooting. One minute I was shooting, and then everything when blank. Now that I see you, I can see that you are all right. Did everyone else do fine?"

"Yes, Audrey. Everyone is okay. I just had a flesh wound, and Tom took care of that. Mason was the one who tried to kill you after knocking me down. When you fell, I stood back up and shot him full of holes. He is dead and gone. He will never be able to hurt anyone again, ever!"

After that day, we spent many hours talking and enjoying the time we had together. I spent more time with Audrey than doing any work. After three weeks, Audrey was up, walking around a little bit every day, getting stronger.

During that time, I was able to fill in the details of all the time we had been apart. With Audrey up and about, I found myself being restless and kind of antsy. I just could not sit around, so I asked Mr. Brand what I could be doing.

"Matt, you showed me before that you are a top hand when it comes to cattle and horses. You know what needs to be done, and you don't need me to tell you what to do. You just need a push, and you'll be the groove. Ask Mr. Parks, he knows what needs to be done.

The other boys know who you are and what you can do, so there is no worry with them."

"By the by, that horse of yours is trying to get to every mare in the pasture. We had to bring him in and put him in a stall for the mares and our own protection. Maybe go see how he is doing, and you can work out some kinks with that big boy."

It was a day later that I found Audrey sitting on the porch. She was in the shade and looking so beautiful. There was still a dark cloud hanging over my head. This was something that had happened just a few days after the massacre and after her being shot. I had to get this off my chest. Now was the time.

"You remember a week or so back. You heard two gunshots and later asked me what had happened. Well, I didn't tell you because of what happened. What happened was between me and another young fella. He came to the ranch, looking for me."

"Why in the world would he be looking for you?"

"Well, it was because I am that guy, Matt Guns, the fast draw guy. That's the name I gained out west. I'm the man who killed Cherokee Lane, Zach Mason, and so many others. This young man came to prove he was faster than me. His problem was he was just way too slow. I tried everything I could do to get him to stop and ride away. I even tried to turn my back on him to walk away, and he drew on me anyway. There was nothing else I could do but to kill or be killed. What he did prove was just how dumb he was. And then he was dead!"

"Well, Matt, you had to do what you had to do. I'm not angry at all. I'm actually glad. You could have been killed, and then I would have been tracking this man down and killing him myself!"

"Yes, but it still hurts me knowing that if one could find me here, how many more will come to try their hand against mine. I just do not know what to do!"

"You were right, Matt. I love you, and I do not want to lose you to some crazy man who wants to try to kill you to prove something."

"Yes, but you know that from Tennessee to Colorado and back, I did what I had to do to stay alive while trying to find Pa and the sisters. I did not go out to gain a reputation. But I've got one regardless. It'll only bring you and your family and mine more tragedy and heartache. I don't want to kill anymore, but I also don't want to die. That's why I'm going to leave for a time. There must be somewhere out there that I can lose myself and lose this reputation. Matt Guns must die so that only Matt Allison can live. This will be hard for you and me, but this is what must be done. If you must, make a new life for yourself, with someone else, not me. It will hurt, but I will never ask for you to wait for me. You do understand what I am saying, don't you?"

"Do you have some doubts about your feelings for me, Matt?"

"No, never! But I also won't ask you to wait around for me until this cloud goes away. I want to settle down the right way so things can be peaceful. Again, if you find somebody you can love better than me then you had best tie the knot with him. You might have to wait a long time for me to come back. Who's to say that I may never will. I could die out there, and you will never know it."

"Yes, I will know, Matt. I will know!"

We spent several hours there on the porch as I gently held her in my arms until the sun set and the moon was just showing in the night sky. I stooped to pick her up with the idea to carry her up to her room when she wrapped her arms around my neck and pulled me into a kiss with such passion and tenderness that was beyond anything that ever happened between us. I knew then that I would never be able to forget that moment. She knew without my saying it because she said it first. "Come back to me soon! I will always love only you! Just come back!"

Chapter 30

The next morning, the sun was burning the haze away from the sky, and the day was going to be a warm one. I had already saddled Duke, and I could see that Pa and the rest of the family were all up to see me off.

As I walked out on the porch, I saw that Duke was all saddled up and Clyde was there with all the gear I would need packed on his back.

"That mule doesn't know how to act without you around him. I swear that mule can understand every word you ever say to him. Tom and I decided that you have to take him with you just to make that mule feel good!"

That was why his load was packed and ready to go. His load wasn't very heavy since I wasn't expecting to go to a war or the likes.

They all knew that I was no good with long goodbyes. My own plan had been to just slip off and let them know where I landed. But there they were, the whole bunch, even the Parks and Mr. Brand showed up.

"I knew that you would try to get away without saying good-byes, so we come out to say our own goodbyes. You need to be careful, son. Don't let anybody sneak up on you or be clumsy. We all love you, but we also know what you are doing and why. Let us know where you finally land. Reputations like yours are hard to get and even harder to get rid of. Just be careful and know we love you. Come back soon if you can. If not, send us a letter sometime. Just let us know where you are!" That was Pa.

Pa and I stood there, and I went to shake his hand. Instead, he pulled me into his arms for a hug. That was only the second time that had happened.

"Be careful, boy. Be safe!"

With a short goodbye and a short kiss from Audrey, there was nothing else to be said. Audrey and I had said our proper goodbyes the night before. I pulled myself into the saddle and gave them all a wave goodbye. I just hoped that Audrey would understand what I was doing. She said she did understand, but I still worried.

My first thought was to head east to Fort Gibson or Fort Smith in Arkansas, but then I changed my mind.

I leaned over and whispered into Duke's ear, "Let's go west!" Clyde snorted once and picked up the pace.

It was time for a new trail to follow. Maybe to Texas or somewhere in the west. Only the good Lord knows where I might end up. But hopefully, it would be a safe place, but I was ready for whatever could or would happen!

The end, but there is always more.

About the Author

Jennifer Kuehnhold
Photography

Elijah Brunson is a true American patriot. He is of a mixed ancestry: Cherokee, Irish, Dutch, English and Swede. He was born in Deming, New Mexico in 1949. From three to sixteen he lived in Inola, Oklahoma. His Brunson pioneer family was made up of farmers, builders, teachers, preachers and politicians.

Elijah, himself, is a retired teacher, preacher, mechanic, carpenter and even tried his hand at selling cars!

While growing up in Oklahoma, he worked with his grandfather and father building homes, hauling hay, riding horses, playing basketball and his favorite sport, baseball!

He earned BA's in American/World History, Language Arts, along with endorsements in Special Education, Drivers Ed and coaching (basketball and baseball at the high school level).

Elijah and his wife Janice of forty-four years have two sons, three daughters, along with seven granddaughters and one grandson!

CPSIA information can be obtained
at www.ICGtesting.com
Printed in the USA
FFHW021107080319
50942150-56356FF